THE STORIES

OF THE

THREE BURGLARS

BY

FRANK R. STOCKTON

NEW YORK
DODD, MEAD AND COMPANY
PUBLISHERS

THE STORIES

OF THE

THREE BURGLARS.

———◆———

I AM a householder in a pleasant country neighbourhood, about twenty miles
from New York. My family consists of
myself and wife, our boy, George William,
aged two, two maid-servants, and a man;
but in the summer we have frequent visit-
ors, and at the time of which I am about
to write my Aunt Martha was staying
with us.

My house is large and pleasant, and we
have neighbours near enough for social
purposes and yet not too near or too many
to detract from the rural aspect of our surroundings. But we do not live in a para-
dise; we are occasionally troubled by
mosquitoes and burglars.

Against the first of these annoyances
we have always been able to guard our-

selves, at least in a measure, and our man and the cook declare that they have become so used to them that they do not mind them; but to guard against burglars is much more difficult, and to become used to them would, I think, require a great deal of practice.

For several months before the period of this narrative our neighbourhood had been subject to visits from burglars. From time to time houses had been entered and robbed, and the offenders had never been detected.

We had no police force, not even a village organization. There was a small railway station near our house, and six miles away was the county town. For fire and police protection each household was obliged to depend upon itself.

Before the beginning of the burglarious enterprises in our midst, we had not felt the need of much protection in this direction; sometimes poultry was stolen, but this was a rare occurrence, and, although windows and doors were generally fastened for the night, this labour was often considered much more troublesome than necessary. But now a great change had taken place in the feelings of our com-

munity. When the first robbery occurred
the neighbours were inclined to laugh about
it, and to say that Captain Hubbard's habit
of sitting up after the rest of his family
had gone to bed and then retiring and for-
getting to close the front door had invited
the entrance of a passing tramp. But
when a second and a third house, where
windows and doors had not been left open,
had been entered, and, in a measure, de-
spoiled, people ceased to laugh; and if
there had been any merriment at all on
the subject, it would have been caused by
the extraordinary and remarkable precautions taken against the entrance of thieves
by night. The loaded pistol became the
favourite companion of the head of the
house; those who had no watch-dogs
bought them; there were new locks, new
bolts, new fastenings. At one time there
was a mounted patrol of young men,
which, however, was soon broken up by
their mothers. But this trouble was unavailing, for at intervals the burglaries
continued.

As a matter of course a great many
theories were broached as to the reasons
for this disturbance in our hitherto peaceful neighbourhood. We were at such a

distance from the ordinary centres of crime that it was generally considered that professional burglars would hardly take the trouble to get to us or to get away from us, and that, therefore, the offences were probably committed by unsuspected persons living in this part of the country who had easy means of determining which houses were worth breaking into and what method of entrance would be most feasible. In this way some families, hitherto regarded as respectable families, had fallen under suspicion.

So far, mine was the only house of any importance within the distance of a mile from the station which had not in some way suffered from burglars. In one or two of these cases the offenders had been frightened away before they had done any other injury than the breaking of a window-shutter; but we had been spared any visitation whatever. After a time we began to consider that this was an invidious distinction. Of course we did not desire that robbers should break into our house and steal, but it was a sort of implied insult that robbers should think that our house was not worth breaking into. We contrived, however, to bear up under this implied contempt and even under the facetious imputations of some of our lively neighbours, who declared that it looked very suspicious that we should lose nothing, and even continue to add to our worldly goods, while everybody else was suffering from abstractions.

I did not, however, allow any relaxation in my vigilance in the protection of my house and family. My time to suffer had not yet arrived, and it might not arrive at all; but if it did come it should not be my fault. I therefore carefully examined all the new precautions my neighbours had taken against the entrance of thieves, and where I approved of them I adopted them.

Of some of these my wife and I did not approve. For instance, a tin pan containing iron spoons, the dinner bell, and a miscellaneous collection of hardware balanced on the top stair of the staircase, and so connected with fine cords that a thief coming up the stairs would send it rattling and bounding to the bottom, was looked upon by us with great disfavour. The descent of the pan, whether by innocent accident or the approach of a burglar, might throw our little boy into a fit, to say nothing of the terrible fright it would give my Aunt Martha, who was a maiden lady of middle age, and not accustomed to a clatter in the night. A bull-dog in the house my wife would not have, nor, indeed, a dog of any kind. George William was not yet old enough to play with dogs, especially a sharp one; and if the dog was not sharp it was of no use to have him in the house. To the ordinary burglar-alarm she strongly objected. She had been in houses where these things went off of their own accord, occasioning great consternation; and, besides, she said that if thieves got into the house she did not want to know it and she did not want me to know it; the quicker they found what they came for and went away with it the better. Of course, she wished them kept out, if such a thing were possible; but if they did get in, our duty as parents of the dearest little boy was non-interference. She insisted, however, that the room in which the loveliest of children slept, and which was also occupied by ourselves, should be made absolutely burglar proof; and this object, by means of extraordinary bolts and chains, I flattered myself I accomplished. My Aunt Martha had a patent contrivance for fastening a door that she always used, whether at home or travelling, and in whose merit she placed implicit confidence. Therefore we did not feel it necessary to be anxious about her; and the servants slept at the top of the house, where thieves would not be likely to go.

"They may continue to slight us by their absence," said my wife, "but I do not believe that they will be able to frighten us by their presence."

I was not, however, so easily contented as my wife. Of course I wished to do everything possible to protect George William and the rest of the family, but I was also very anxious to protect our property in all parts of the house. Therefore, in addition to everything else I had done, I devised a scheme for interfering with the plans of men who should feloniously break into our home.

After a consultation with a friend, who was a physician greatly interested in the study of narcotic drugs, I procured a mixture which was almost tasteless and without peculiar odour, and of which a small quantity would in less than a minute throw an ordinary man into a state of unconsciousness. The potion was, however, no more dangerous in its effects than that quantity of ardent spirits which would cause entire insensibility. After the lapse of several hours, the person under the influence of the drug would recover consciousness without assistance. But in order to provide against all contingencies my friend prepared a powerful antidote, which would almost immediately revive one who had been made unconscious by our potion.

The scheme that I had devised may possibly have been put into use by others. But of this I know not. I thought it a good scheme and determined to experiment with it, and, if possible, to make a trap which should catch a burglar. I would reveal this plan to no one but my friend the physician and my wife. Secrecy would be an important element in its success.

Our library was a large and pleasant room on the ground floor of the house, and here I set my trap. It was my habit to remain in this room an hour or so after the rest of the family had gone to bed, and, as I was an early riser, I was always in it again before it was necessary for a servant to enter it in the morning.

Before leaving the library for the night

I placed in a conspicuous position in the room a small table, on which was a tray holding two decanters partially filled with wine, in the one red and in the other white. There was also upon the tray an open box of biscuit and three wine-glasses, two of them with a little wine at the bottom. I took pains to make it appear that these refreshments had been recently partaken of. There were biscuit crumbs upon the tray, and a drop or two of wine was freshly spilled upon it every time the trap was set. The table, thus arranged, was left in the room during the night, and early in the morning I put the tray and its contents into a closet and locked it up.

A portion of my narcotic preparation was thoroughly mixed with the contents of each of the decanters in such proportions that a glass of the wine would be sufficient to produce the desired effect.

It was my opinion that there were few men who, after a night walk and perhaps some labour in forcibly opening a door or a window-shutter, would not cease for a moment in pursuance of their self-imposed task to partake of the refreshments so conveniently left behind them by the occupants of the house when they retired to rest. Should my surmises be correct, I might reasonably expect, should my house be broken into, to find an unconscious burglar in the library when I went down in the morning. And I was sure, and my wife agreed with me, that if I should find a burglar in that room or any other part of the house, it was highly desirable that he should be an unconscious one.

Night after night I set my burglar trap, and morning after morning I locked it up in the closet. I cannot say that I was exactly disappointed that no opportunity offered to test the value of my plan, but it did seem a pity that I should take so much trouble for nothing. It had been some weeks since any burglaries had been committed in the neighbourhood, and it was the general opinion that the miscreants had considered this field worked out and had transferred their labours to a better-paying place. The insult of having been considered unworthy the attention of the knights of the midnight jimmy remained with us, but as all our goods and chattels also remained with us we could afford to brook the indignity.

As the trap cost nothing my wife did not object to my setting it every night for the present. Something might happen, she remarked, and it was just as well to be prepared in more ways than one; but there was a point upon which she was very positive.

"When George William is old enough to go about the house by himself," she said, "those decanters must not be left exposed upon the table. Of course I do not expect him to go about the house drinking wine and everything that he finds, but there is no knowing what a child in the first moments of his investigative existence may do."

For myself, I became somewhat tired of acting my part in this little farce every night and morning, but when I have undertaken anything of this sort I am slow to drop it.

It was about three weeks since I had begun to set my trap when I was awakened in the night by a sudden noise. I sat up in bed, and as I did so my wife said to me sleepily, —

"What is that? Was it thunder? There it is again!" she exclaimed, starting up. "What a crash! It must have struck somewhere." I did not answer. It was not thunder. It was something in the house, and it flashed into my mind that perhaps my trap had been sprung. I got out of bed and began rapidly to dress.

"What are you going to do?" anxiously asked my wife.

"I'm going to see what has happened," said I. At that moment there was another noise. This was like two or three heavy footsteps, followed by a sudden thump; but it was not so loud as the others.

"John," cried my wife, "don't stir an inch, it's burglars!" and she sprang out of bed and seized me by the arm.

"I must go down," I said; "but there is really no reason for your being frightened. I shall call David, and shall carry my pistol, so there is really no danger. If there are thieves in the house they have probably decamped by this time — that is, if they are able to do so, for of course they must know that noise would awaken the soundest sleepers."

My wife looked at me and then slowly withdrew her hands from my arm.

"You promise me," she said, "if you find a burglar downstairs in the possession of his senses you will immediately come back to me and George William?"

I promised her, and, slipping on some clothes, I went out into the second-story hall. I carried no light. Before I had reached the bottom of the back stairs I heard David, my man, coming down. To be sure it was he and not a burglar I spoke to him in a low voice, my pistol raised in case of an unsatisfactory reply.

"I heard that noise, sir," he whispered, "and was going down to see about it."

"Are you ready if it's thieves?" I whispered.

"I have got the biscuit-beater," he replied.

"Come on, then," said I, and we went downstairs.

I had left no light in the library, but there was one there now, and it shone through the open door into the hallway. We stopped and listened. There was no sound, and then slowly and cautiously we approached the door of the library. The scene I beheld astounded me, and involuntarily I sprang back a step or two. So did David; but in an instant we saw that there was no need of retreat or defence. Stretched upon the floor, not far from the doorway, lay a tall man, his face upturned to the light of a bull's-eye lantern which stood by the mantel-piece. His eyes were shut, and it was evident that he was perfectly insensible. Near by, in the wreck of the small table, glasses, and decanters, lay another man, apparently of heavier build. He also was as still as a corpse. A little further back, half sitting on the floor, with the upper part of his body resting against the lounge, was another man with a black mask over his face.

"Are they dead?" exclaimed David, in an undertone of horror.

"No," said I, "they are not dead; they have been caught in my trap."

And I must admit that the consciousness of this created a proud exultation of spirit within me. I had overmatched these rascals; they were prostrated before me. If one of them moved, David and I could kill him. But I did not believe there would be any killing, nor any moving for the present.

In a high whisper, which could have been heard distinctly all over the house, my wife now called to me from the top of the stairs. "What is it?" she said. "What has happened?"

I stepped quickly to the stairway.

"Everything is all right," I said in a

loud, distinct voice, intended to assure my wife that there was no necessity for caution or alarm. "I will be with you presently."

"I am glad to hear that nothing is the matter," said Aunt Martha, now for the first time opening her door. "I was afraid something had happened."

But I had business to attend to before I could go upstairs. In thinking over and arranging this plan for the capture of burglars, I had carefully considered its various processes, and had provided against all the contingencies I could think of; therefore I was not now obliged to deliberate what I should do. "Keep your eye on them," said I to David, "and if one of them moves be ready for him. The first thing to do is to tie them hand and foot."

I quickly lighted a lamp, and then took from another shelf of the closet a large coil of strong cotton rope, which I had provided for such an occasion as the present.

"Now," said I to David, "I will tie them while you stand by to knock over any one of them who attempts to get up."

The instrument with which David was

prepared to carry out my orders was a
formidable one. In the days of my youth
my family was very fond of " Maryland
biscuit," which owes much of its delicacy
to the fact that before baking it is pounded
and beaten by a piece of heavy iron. Some
people used one kind of a beater and
some another, but we had had made for
the purpose a heavy iron club a little over
a foot long, large and heavy at one end
and a handle at the other. In my present
household Maryland biscuits were never
made, but I had preserved this iron beater
as a memento of my boyhood, and when
the burglaries began in our vicinity I gave
it to David to keep in his room, to be
used as a weapon if necessary. I did not
allow him to have a pistol, having a regard
for my own safety in a sudden night alarm,
and nothing could be more formidable in
a hand-to-hand encounter than this skull-
crushing club.

I began with the tall man, and rapidly
tied his feet together with many twists of
the rope and as many knots. I then
turned him over and tied his elbows behind him in the same secure way. I had
given so much thought to the best method
of securing a man by cords, that I do not

think this fellow could possibly have released himself when I had finished with
him.

David was obeying my orders and keeping a strict watch on the prostrate men;
but his emotions of amazement were so
great that he could not keep them down.

"What is the matter with them, sir?"
he said. "How did they come so?"

"There is no time for talking now," I
answered. "I will tell you all about it
when the men have been secured." I now
turned my attention to the man who was
partly resting against the lounge. I first
tied his feet, and before letting him down
to the floor, so as to get to his arms, I removed his hat and his mask, which was
made of black muslin. I was surprised to
see the beardless face of a young and very
good-looking man. He was well dressed,
and had the general appearance of a person belonging to theatrical circles. When
his arms had been tied, I told David he
might lay down his biscuit-beater, and
help me with the third man, who was
badly mixed up with the *débris* of the refreshments. We hauled him out and tied
him up. He was rather a short man, but
very heavy, and I could see no signs of his

having been hurt by the smash-up he made in falling.

We now proceeded to search the insensible burglars for arms. Upon the tall man we found a large revolver, a heavy billy, which seemed as if it had seen service, and a long-bladed knife. The stout man carried two double-barrelled pistols, and upon one of the fingers of his right hand wore a brass ring with a murderous-looking iron protuberance upon it, which, when driven forward by his powerful arm, was probably more dangerous than a billy. Upon the younger man we found no arms at all, and his hip pocket contained nothing but a small handbook on civil engineering.

I now briefly explained to David the nature of the trap which had caught the burglars. He gazed upon me with a face glowing with amazed admiration.

"What a head you have got, sir!" he exclaimed. "I don't believe there is another man in this State who would have thought of that. And what are you going to do with them now, sir; hang 'em? That's what ought to be done with them, the hounds!"

"All I shall do," I answered, "will be to keep them till daylight, and then I shall send word to the sheriff at Kennertown, and have him send officers for them."

"Upon my word," exclaimed David, "they are in the worst kind of a box."

Now my wife called me again. "What in the world are you doing down there?" she called; "why don't you come up-stairs?"

This annoyed me, for I was not yet ready to go upstairs. I wished to resuscitate these fellows, for their stupor was so profound that I began to fear that perhaps they had taken too much of the drug and ought to be brought to their senses as speedily as possible. This feeling was due more to my desire that serious injuries should not occur to the rascals while in my house than to any concern for them.

"My dear," said I, stepping to the bottom of the stairs, "I have some things to attend to down here which will occupy me a few minutes longer; then I will come up to you."

"I can't imagine what the things are," she said, "but I suppose I can wait," and she went into her room and closed her door after her.

I now began to consider what was to be done with the burglars after they had been resuscitated. My first impulse was to rid the house of them by carrying them out of doors and bringing them to their senses there. But there was an objection to this plan. They would be pretty heavy fellows to carry, and as it would be absolutely necessary to watch them until they could be given into the charge of the officers of the law, I did not want to stay out of doors to do this, for the night air was raw and chilly, and I therefore determined to keep them in the house. And as they could be resuscitated better in a sitting position, they must be set up in some way or other. I consulted David on the subject.

"You might put 'em up with their backs agin the wall, sir," said he, "but the dirty beasts would spoil the paper. I wouldn't keep them in a decent room like this. I'd haul 'em out into the kitchen, anyway."

But as they were already in the library I decided to let them stay there, and to get them as speedily as possible into some position in which they might remain. I bethought me of a heavy wooden settle or bench with back and arms which stood on the side piazza. With David's help I brought this into the room and placed it with its back to the window.

"Now, then," said I to David, "we will put them on this bench, and I will tie them fast to it. We cannot be too careful in securing them, for if one of them were to get loose, even without arms, there is no knowing what trouble he might make."

"Well, sir," said David, "if I'm to handle them at all, I'd rather have them dead, as I hope they are, than have them alive; but you needn't be afraid, sir, that any one of them will get loose. If I see any signs of that I'll crack the rascal's skull in a jiffy."

It required a great deal of tugging and lifting to get those three men on the bench, but we got them there side by side, their heads hanging listlessly, some one way, some another. I then tied each one of them firmly to the bench.

I had scarcely finished this when I again heard my wife's voice from the top of the stairs.

"If any pipes have burst," she called down, "tell David not to catch the water in the new milk-pans."

"Very well," I replied, "I'll see to it," and was rejoiced to hear again the shutting of the bedroom door.

I now saturated a sponge with the powerful preparation which Dr. Marks had prepared as an antidote, and held it under the nose of the tall burglar. In less than twenty seconds he made a slight quivering in his face as if he were about to sneeze, and very soon he did sneeze slightly. Then he sneezed violently, raised his head, and opened his eyes. For a moment he gazed blankly before him, and then looked stupidly at David and at me. But in an instant there flashed into his face the look of a wild beast. His quick, glittering eye took in the whole situation at a glance. With a furious oath he threw himself forward with such a powerful movement that he nearly lifted the bench.

"Stop that," said David, who stood near him with his iron club uplifted. "If you do that again I'll let you feel this."

The man looked at him with a fiery flash in his eyes, and then he looked at me, as I stood holding the muzzle of my pistol within two feet of his face. The black and red faded out of his countenance. He became pale. He glanced at his companions bound and helpless. His expression now changed entirely. The fury of the wild beast was succeeded by a look of frightened subjection. Gazing very anxiously at my pistol, he said, in a voice which, though agitated, was low and respectful : —

" What does this mean ? What are you going to do ? Will you please turn away the muzzle of that pistol ? "

I took no notice of this indication of my steadiness of hand, and answered : —

" I am going to bring these other scoundrels to their senses, and early in the morning the three of you will be on your way to jail, where I hope you may remain for the rest of your lives."

" If you don't get killed on your way there," said David, in whose nervous hand the heavy biscuit-beater was almost as dangerous as my pistol.

The stout man who sat in the middle of the bench was twice as long in reviving as had been his companion, who watched the operation with intense interest. When the burly scoundrel finally became conscious, he sat for a few minutes gazing at the floor with a silly grin ; then he raised his head and looked first at one of his companions and then at the other, gazed for an instant at me and David, tried to move his feet, gave a pull at one arm and

then at the other, and when he found
he was bound hard and fast, his face
turned as red as fire and he opened
his mouth, whether to swear or yell I
know not. I had already closed the door,
and before the man had uttered more than
a premonitory sound, David had clapped
the end of his bludgeon against his mouth.

" Taste that," he said, " and you know
what you will get if you disturb this
family with any of your vile cursin' and
swearin'."

" Look here," said the tall man, suddenly turning to the other with an air of
authority, " keep your mouth shut and
don't speak till you're spoken to. Mind
that, now, or these gentlemen will make
it the worse for you."

David grinned as he took away his
club.

" I'd gentlemen you," he said, " if I
could get half a chance to do it."

The face of the heavy burglar main-
tained its redness, but he kept his mouth
shut.

When the younger man was restored to
his senses, his full consciousness and power
of perception seemed to come to him in an
instant. His eyes flashed from right to

left, he turned deadly white, and then merely moving his arms and legs enough to make himself aware that he was bound, he sat perfectly still and said not a word.

I now felt that I must go and acquaint my wife with what had happened, or otherwise she would be coming downstairs to see what was keeping me so long. David declared that he was perfectly able to keep guard over them, and I ran upstairs. David afterward told me that as soon as I left the room the tall burglar endeavoured to bribe him to cut their ropes, and told him if he was afraid to stay behind after doing this he would get him a much better situation than this could possibly be. But as David threatened personal injury to the speaker if he uttered another word of the kind, the tall man said no more ; but the stout man became very violent and angry, threatening all sorts of vengeance on my unfortunate man. David said he was beginning to get angry, when the tall man, who seemed to have much influence over the other fellow, ordered him to keep quiet, as the gentleman with the iron club no doubt thought he was doing right. The young fellow never said a word.

When I told my wife that I had caught three burglars, and they were fast bound in the library, she nearly fainted; and when I had revived her she begged me to promise that I would not go downstairs again until the police had carried away the horrible wretches. But I assured her that it was absolutely necessary for me to return to the library. She then declared that she would go with me, and if anything happened she would share my fate. "Besides," she said, " if they are tied fast so they can't move, I should like to see what they look like. I never saw a burglar."

I did not wish my wife to go downstairs, but as I knew there would be no use in objecting, I consented. She hastily dressed herself, making me wait for her; and when she left the room she locked the door on the sleeping George William, in order that no one should get at him during her absence. As we passed the head of the stairs, the door of my Aunt Martha's room opened, and there she stood, completely dressed, with her bonnet on, and a little leather bag in her hand.

"I heard so much talking and so much going up and down stairs that I thought I had better be ready to do whatever had to be done. Is it fire?"

"No," said my wife; "it's three burglars tied in a bunch in the library. I am going down to see them."

My Aunt Martha gasped, and looked as if she were going to sit down on the floor.

"Goodness gracious!" she said, "if you're going I'll go too. I can't let you go alone, and I never did see a burglar."

I hurried down and left the two ladies on the stairs until I was sure everything was still safe; and when I saw that there had been no change in the state of affairs, I told them to come down.

When my wife and Aunt Martha timidly looked in at the library door, the effect upon them and the burglars was equally interesting. The ladies each gave a start and a little scream, and huddled themselves close to me, and the three burglars gazed at them with faces that expressed more astonishment than any I had ever seen before. The stout fellow gave vent to a smothered exclamation, and the face of the young man flushed, but not one of them spoke.

"Are you sure they are tied fast?" whispered my Aunt Martha to me.

"Perfectly," I answered; "if I had not been sure I should not have allowed you to come down."

Thereupon the ladies picked up courage and stepped further into the room.

"Did you and David catch them?" asked my aunt; "and how in the world did you do it?"

"I'll tell you all about that another time," I said, "and you had better go up-stairs as soon as you two have seen what sort of people are these cowardly burglars who sneak or break into the houses of respectable people at night, and rob and steal and ruin other people's property with no more conscience or human feeling than is possessed by the rats which steal your corn, or the polecats which kill your chickens."

"I can scarcely believe," said Aunt Martha, "that that young man is a real burglar."

At these words the eyes of the fellow spoken of glowed as he fixed them on Aunt Martha, but he did not say a word, and the paleness which had returned to his face did not change.

"Have they told you who they are?" asked my wife.

"I haven't asked them," I said. "And now don't you think you had better go up-stairs?"

"It seems to me," said Aunt Martha, "that those ropes must hurt them."

The tall man now spoke. "Indeed they do, madam," he said in a low voice and very respectful manner, "they are very tight."

I told David to look at all the cords and see if any of them were too tightly drawn.

"It's all nonsense, sir," said he, when he had finished the examination; "not one of the ropes is a bit too tight. All they want is a chance to pull out their ugly hands."

"Of course," said Aunt Martha, "if it would be unsafe to loosen the knots I wouldn't do it. Are they to be sent to prison?"

"Yes," said I; "as soon as the day breaks I shall send down for the police."

I now heard a slight sound at the door, and turning, saw Alice, our maid of the house, who was peeping in at the door. Alice was a modest girl, and quite pretty.

"I heard the noise and the talking, sir," she said, "and when I found the ladies had gone down to see what it was, I thought I would come too."

" And where is the cook," asked my wife ; " don't she want to see burglars ? "

" Not a bit of it," answered Alice, very emphatically. " As soon as I told her what it was she covered up her head with the bedclothes and declared, ma'am, that she would never get up until they were entirely gone out of the house."

At this the stout man grinned.

" I wish you'd all cover up your heads," he said. The tall man looked at him severely, and he said no more.

David did not move from his post near the three burglars, but he turned toward Alice and looked at her. We knew that he had tender feelings toward the girl, and I think that he did not approve of her being there.

" Have they stolen anything ? " asked Aunt Martha.

" They have not had any chance to take anything away," I said; and my wife remarked that whether they had stolen anything or not, they had made a dreadful mess on the floor, and had broken the table. They should certainly be punished.

At this she made a motion as if she would leave the room, and an anxious expression immediately came on the face of the tall man, who had evidently been revolving something in his mind.

"Madam," he said, "we are very sorry that we have broken your table, and that we have damaged some of your glass and your carpet. I assure you, however, that nothing of the kind would have happened but for that drugged wine, which was doubtless intended for a medicine, and not a beverage; but weary and chilled as we were when we arrived, madam, we were glad to partake of it, supposing it ordinary wine."

I could not help showing a little pride at the success of my scheme.

"The refreshment was intended for fellows of your class, and I am very glad you accepted it."

The tall man did not answer me, but he again addressed my wife.

"Madam," he said, "if you ladies would remain and listen to me a few moments, I am sure I would make you aware that there is much to extenuate the apparent offence which I have committed to-night."

My wife did not answer him, but turning to me said, smiling, " If he alludes to their drinking your wine he need not apologize."

The man looked at her with an expression as if her words had pained him.

" Madam," he said, " if you consent to listen to my explanations and the story of this affair, I am sure your feelings toward me would not be so harsh."

" Now, then," said my Aunt Martha, " if he has a story to tell he ought to be allowed to tell it, even in a case like this. Nobody should be judged until he has said what he thinks he ought to say. Let us hear his story."

I laughed. " Any statement he may make," I said, " will probably deserve a much stronger name than stories."

" I think that what you say is true," remarked my wife ; " but still if he has a story to tell I should like to hear it."

I think I heard David give a little grunt ; but he was too well bred to say anything.

" Very well," said I, " if you choose to sit up and hear him talk, it is your affair. I shall be obliged to remain here anyway, and will not object to anything that will help to pass away the time. But these

men must not be the only ones who are
seated. David, you and Alice can clear
away that broken table and the rest of the
stuff, and then we might as well sit down
and make ourselves comfortable."

Alice, with cloth and brush, approached
very timidly the scene of the disaster; but
the younger burglar, who was nearest to
her, gazed upon her with such a gentle and
quiet air that she did not seem to be
frightened. When she and David had put
the room in fair order, I placed two easy-
chairs for my wife and Aunt Martha at a
moderate distance from the burglars, and
took another myself a little nearer to
them, and then told David to seat himself
near the other end of the bench, and Alice
took a chair at a little distance from the
ladies.

"Now, then," said Aunt Martha to the
burglars, "I would like very much to hear
what any one of you can say in extenua-
tion of having broken into a gentleman's
house by night."

Without hesitation the tall man began
his speech. He had a long and rather
lean, close-shaven face, which at present
bore the expression of an undertaker con-
ducting a funeral. Although it was my

aunt who had shown the greatest desire to hear his story, he addressed himself to my wife. I think he imagined that she was the more influential person of the two.

"Madam," said he, "I am glad of the opportunity of giving you and your family an idea of the difficulties and miseries which beset a large class of your fellow-beings of whom you seldom have any chance of knowing anything at all, but of whom you hear all sorts of the most misleading accounts. Now, I am a poor man. I have suffered the greatest miseries that poverty can inflict. I am here, suspected of having committed a crime. It is possible that I may be put to considerable difficulty and expense in proving my innocence."

"I shouldn't wonder," I interrupted. To this remark he paid no attention.

"Considering all this," he continued, "you may not suppose, madam, that as a boy I was brought up most respectably and properly. My mother was a religious woman, and my father was a boat-builder. I was sent to school, and my mother has often told me that I was a good scholar. But she died when I was about sixteen, and I am sure had this not happened I should never have been even suspected of breaking the laws of my country. Not long after her death my father appeared to lose interest in his business, and took to rowing about the river instead of building boats for other people to row. Very often he went out at night, and I used to wonder why he should care to be on the water in the darkness, and sometimes in the rain. One evening at supper he said to me : ' Thomas, you ought to know how to row in the dark as well as in the daytime. I am going up the river to-night, and you can come with me.'

"It was about my ordinary bedtime when we took a boat with two pair of oars, and we pulled up the river about three miles above the city."

"What city?" I asked.

"The city where I was born, sir," he said, "and the name of which I must be excused from mentioning for reasons connected with my only surviving parent. There were houses on the river bank, but they were not very near each other. Some of them had lights in them, but most of them were dark, as it must have been after eleven o'clock. Before one of them my father stopped rowing for a moment and looked at it pretty hard. It seemed to be all dark, but as we pulled on a little I saw a light in the back of the house.

"My father said nothing, but we kept on, though pulling very easy for a mile or two, and then we turned and floated down with the tide. 'You might as well rest, Thomas,' said he, 'for you have worked pretty hard.'

"We floated slowly, for the tide was just beginning to turn, and when we got near the house which I mentioned, I noticed that there was no light in it. When we were about opposite to it father suddenly looked up and said, not speaking very loud, 'By George! if that isn't Williamson Green's house. I wasn't thinking of it when we rowed up, and passed it without taking notice of it. I am sorry for that, for I wanted to see Williamson, and now I expect he has gone to bed.'

"'Who is Mr. Green?' I asked.

"'He is an old friend of mine,' said my father, 'and I haven't seen him for some little while now. About four months ago he borrowed of me a sextant, quadrant, and chronometer. They were instruments I took from old Captain Barney in payment of some work I did for him. I wasn't usin' them, and Williamson had bought a catboat and was studying navigation; but he has given up that fad now and has promised me over and over to send me back my instruments, but he has never done it. If I'd thought of it I would have stopped and got 'em of him; but I didn't think, and now I expect he has gone to bed. However, I'll row in shore and see; perhaps he's up yet.'

"You see, ma'am," said the speaker to my wife, "I'm tellin' you all these particulars because I am very anxious you should understand exactly how everything happened on this night, which was the turning-point of my life."

"Very good," said Aunt Martha; "we want to hear all the particulars."

"Well, then," continued the burglar, "we pulled up to a stone wall which was at the bottom of Green's place and made fast, and father he got out and went up to the house. After a good while he came back and said that he was pretty sure Williamson Green had gone to bed, and as it wouldn't do to waken people up from their sleep to ask them for nautical instruments they had borrowed, he sat down for a minute on the top of the wall, and then he slapped his knee, not making much noise, though.

"'By George!' he said, 'an idea has just struck me. I can play the prettiest trick on Williamson that ever was played on mortal man. Those instruments are all in a box locked up, and I know just where he keeps it. I saw it not long ago, when I went to his house to talk about a yacht he wants built. They are on a table in the corner of his bedroom. He was taking me through the house to show me the improvements he had made, and he said to me : —

"'"Martin, there's your instruments. I won't trouble you to take them with you, because they're heavy and you're not going straight home, but I'll bring them to you day after to-morrow, when I shall be goin' your way."

"'Now, then,' said my father, 'the trick I'm thinkin' of playing on Williamson is this: I'd like to take that box of instruments out of his room without his knowing it and carry them home, having the boat here convenient; and then in a day or two to write to him and tell him I must have 'em, because I have a special use for 'em. Of course he'll be awfully cut up, not having them to send back; and when he comes down to my place to talk about it, and after hearing all he has to say, I'll show him the box. He'll be the most dumbfoundedest man in this State; and if I don't choose to tell him he'll never know to his dying day how I got that box. And if he lies awake at night, trying to think how I got it, it will serve him right for keeping my property from me so long.'

"'But, father,' said I, 'if the people have gone to bed you can't get into the house to play him your trick.'

"'That can be managed,' says he; 'I'm rather old for climbing myself, but I know a way by which you, Thomas, can get in easy enough. At the back of the house is a trellis with a grape-vine running over it, and the top of it is just under one of the second-story windows. You can climb up that trellis, Thomas, and lift up that window-sash very carefully, so's not to make no noise, and get in. Then you'll be in a back room, with a door right in front of you which opens into Mr. and Mrs. Green's bedroom. There's always a little night lamp burning in it, by which you can see to get about. In the corner, on your right as you go into the room, is a table with my instrument-box standing on it. The box is pretty heavy, and there is a handle on top to carry it by. You needn't be afraid to go in, for by this time they are both sound asleep, and you can pick up the box and walk out as gingerly as a cat, having of course taken your shoes off before you went in. Then you can hand the box out the back window to me, — I can climb up high enough to reach it, — and you can scuttle down, and we'll be off, having the best rig on Williamson Green that I ever heard of in my born days.'

"I was a very active boy, used to climbing and all that sort of thing, and I had no doubt that I could easily get into the house; but I did not fancy my father's scheme.

"'Suppose,' I said, 'that Mr. Williamson Green should wake up and see me; what could I say? How could I explain my situation?'

"'You needn't say anything,' said my father. 'If he wakes up blow out the light and scoot. If you happen to have the box in your hand drop it out the back window and then slip down after it. He won't see us; but if he does he cannot catch us before we get to the boat; but if he should, however, I'll have to explain the matter to him, and the joke will be against me; but I shall get my instruments, which is the main point, after all.'

"I did not argue with my father, for he was a man who hated to be differed with, and I agreed to help him carry out his little joke. We took off our shoes and walked quietly to the back of the house. My father stood below, and I climbed up the trellis under the back window, which he pointed out. The window-sash was down all but a little crack to let in air, and I raised it so slowly and gently that I made no noise. Then without any trouble at all I got into the room.

"I found myself in a moderate-sized chamber, into which a faint light came from a door opposite the window. Having been several hours out in the night my eyes had become so accustomed to darkness that this light was comparatively strong and I could see everything.

"Looking about me my eyes fell on a little bedstead, on which lay one of the most beautiful infants I ever beheld in my life. Its golden hair lay in ringlets upon the pillow. Its eyes were closed, but its soft cheeks had in them a rosy tinge which almost equalled the colour of its dainty little lips, slightly opened as it softly breathed and dreamed." At this point I saw my wife look quickly at the bedroom key she had in her hand. I knew she was thinking of George William.

"I stood entranced," continued the burglar, "gazing upon this babe, for I was very fond of children; but I remembered that I must not waste time, and stepped softly into the next room. There I beheld Mr. and Mrs. Williamson Green in bed, both fast asleep, the gentleman breathing a little hard. In a corner, just where my father told me I should find it, stood the box upon the table.

"But I could not immediately pick it up and depart. The beautiful room in which I found myself was a revelation to me. Until that moment I had not known that I had tastes and sympathies of a higher order than might have been expected of the youthful son of a boat-builder. Those artistic furnishings aroused within a love of the beautiful which I did not know I possessed. The carpets, the walls, the pictures, the hangings in the windows, the furniture, the ornaments, — everything, in fact, impressed me with such a delight that I did not wish to move or go away.

"Into my young soul there came a longing. 'Oh!' I said to myself, 'that my parents had belonged to the same social grade as that worthy couple reposing in that bed; and oh! that I, in my infancy, had been as beautiful and as likely to be so carefully nurtured and cultured as that sweet babe in the next room.' I almost heaved a sigh as I thought of the difference between these surroundings and my own, but I checked myself; it would not do to made a noise and spoil my father's joke.

"There were a great many things in that luxurious apartment which it would have delighted me to look upon and examine, but I forbore.

"I wish I'd been there," said the stout man; "there wouldn't have been any forbearin'."

The speaker turned sharply upon him.

"Don't you interrupt me again," he

said angrily. Then, instantly resuming his deferential tone, he continued the story.

"But I had come there by the command of my parent, and this command must be obeyed without trifling or loss of time. My father did not approve of trifling or loss of time. I moved quietly toward the table in the corner, on which stood my father's box. I was just about to put my hand upon it when I heard a slight movement behind me. I gave a start and glanced backward. It was Mr. Williamson Green turning over in his bed; what if he should awake? His back was now toward me, and my impulse was to fly and leave everything behind me; but my father had ordered me to bring the box, and he expected his orders to be obeyed. I had often been convinced of that.

"I stood perfectly motionless for a minute or so, and when the gentleman recommenced his regular and very audible breathing I felt it safe to proceed with my task. Taking hold of the box I found it was much heavier than I expected it to be; but I moved gently away with it and passed into the back room.

"There I could not refrain from stop-ying a moment by the side of the sleeping babe, upon whose cherub-like face the light of the night lamp dimly shone. The little child was still sleeping sweetly, and my impulse was to stop and kiss it ; but I knew that this would be wrong. The infant might awake and utter a cry and my father's joke be spoiled. I moved to the open window, and with some trouble, and, I think, without any noise, I succeeded in getting out upon the trellis with the box under my arm. The descent was awkward, but my father was a tall man, and, reaching upward, relieved me of my burden before I got to the ground.

"'I didn't remember it was so heavy,' he whispered, ' or I should have given you a rope to lower it down by. If you had dropped it and spoiled my instruments, and made a lot of noise besides, I should have been angry enough.'

"I was very glad my father was not angry, and following him over the greensward we quickly reached the boat, where the box was stowed away under the bow to keep it from injury.

"We pushed off as quietly as possible and rowed swiftly down the river. When we had gone about a mile I suddenly dropped my oar with an exclamation of dismay.

"'What's the matter?' cried my father.

"'Oh, I have done a dreadful thing!' I said. 'Oh, father, I must go back!'

"I am sorry to say that at this my father swore.

"'What do you want to go back for?' he said.

"'Just to think of it! I have left open the window in which that beautiful child was sleeping. If it should take cold and die from the damp air of the river blowing upon it I should never forgive myself. Oh, if I had only thought of climbing up the trellis again and pulling down that sash! I am sure I could go back and do it without making the least noise.' My father gave a grunt; but what the grunt meant I do not know, and for a few moments he was silent, and then he said: —

"'Thomas, you cannot go back; the distance is too great, the tide is against us, and it is time that you and I were both in our beds. Nothing may happen to that baby; but, attend to my words now, if any harm should come to that child it will go hard with you. If it should die it would be of no use for you to talk about practical jokes. You would be held responsible for its death. I was going to say to you that it might be as well for you not to say anything about this little venture until I had seen how Williamson Green took the joke. Some people get angry with very little reason, although I hardly believe he's that sort of a man; but now things are different. He thinks all the world of that child, which is the only one they've got; and if you want to stay outside of jail or the house of refuge I warn you never to say a word of where you have been this night.'

"With this he began to row again, and I followed his example, but with a very heavy heart. All that night I dreamt of the little child with the damp night winds blowing in upon it."

"Did you ever hear if it caught cold?" asked Aunt Martha.

"No," replied the burglar, "I never did. I mentioned the matter to my father, and he said that he had great fears upon the subject, for although he had written to Williamson Green, asking him to return the instruments, he had not seen him or heard from him, and he was afraid that the child had died or was dangerously sick. Shortly after that my father sent me on a little trip to the Long Island coast to collect some bills from people for whom he had done work. He gave me money to stay a week or two at the seashore, saying that the change would do me good; and it was while I was away on this delightful holiday that an event occurred which had a most disastrous effect upon my future life. My father was arrested for burglary!

"It appeared — and I cannot tell you how shocked I was when I discovered the truth — that the box which I had carried away did not contain nautical instruments, but was filled with valuable plate and jewels. My unfortunate father heard from a man who had been discharged from the service of the family whose house he had visited — whose name, by the way, was not Green — where the box containing the valuables mentioned was always placed at night, and he had also received accurate information in regard to the situation of the rooms and the best method of gaining access to them.

"I believe that some arrangement had been made between my father and this discharged servant in regard to a division of the contents of the box, and it was on account of a disagreement on this subject that the man became very angry, and after pocketing what my father thought was his fair share he departed to unknown regions, leaving behind a note to the police which led to my father's arrest."

" That was a mean trick," said Aunt Martha.

The burglar looked at her gratefully.

"In the lower spheres of life, madam, such things often happen. Some of the plate and jewels were found in my father's possession, and he was speedily tried and sentenced to a long term of imprisonment. And now, can you imagine, ladies," said the tall burglar, apparently having become satisfied to address himself to Aunt Martha as well as my wife, " the wretched position in which I found myself? I was upbraided as the son of a thief. I soon found myself without home, without occupation, and, alas! without good reputation. I was careful not to mention my voluntary connection with my father's crime for fear that should I do so I might be compelled to make a statement which might increase the severity of his punishment. For this reason I did not dare to make inquiries concerning the child in whom I had taken such an interest, and whose little life I had, perhaps, imperilled. I never knew, ladies, whether that infant grew up or not.

" But I, alas! grew up to a life of hardship and degradation. It would be impossible for persons in your sphere of life to understand what I now was obliged to suffer. Suitable employment I could not obtain, because I was the son of a burglar. With a father in the State prison it was of no use for me to apply for employment at any respectable place of business. I laboured at one thing and another, sometimes engaging in the most menial employments. I also had been educated and brought up by my dear mother for a very different career. Sometimes I managed to live fairly well, sometimes I suffered. Always I suffered from the stigma of my father's crime ; always in the eyes of the community in which I lived — a community, I am sorry to say, incapable, as a rule, of making correct judgments in delicate cases like these — I was looked upon as belonging to the ranks of the dishonest. It was a hard lot, and sometimes almost impossible to bear up under.

"I have spoken at length, ladies, in

order that you may understand my true position; and I wish to say that I have never felt the crushing weight of my father's disgrace more deeply than I felt it last evening. This man," nodding toward the stout burglar, " came to me shortly after I had eaten my supper, which happened to be a frugal one, and said to me : —

" 'Thomas, I have some business to attend to to-night, in which you can help me if you choose. I know you are a good mechanic.'

" 'If it is work that will pay me,' I answered, 'I should be very glad to do it, for I am greatly in need of money.'

" 'It will pay,' said he ; and I agreed to assist him.

" As we were walking to the station, as the business to be attended to was out of town, this man, whose name is James Barlow, talked to me in such a way that I began to suspect that he intended to commit a burglary, and openly charged him with this evil purpose. 'You may call it burglary or anything else you please,' said he; 'property is very unequally divided in this world, and it is my business in life to make wrong things right as far as I can. I am going to the house of a man who has a great deal more than he needs, and I haven't anything like as much as I need; and so I intend to take some of his overplus, — not very much, for when I leave his house he will still be a rich man, and I'll be a poor one. But for a time my family will not starve.'

"'Argue as you please, James Barlow,' I said, 'what you are going to do is nothing less than burglary.'

"'Of course it is,' said he; 'but it's all right, all the same. There are a lot of people, Thomas, who are not as particular about these things as they used to be, and there is no use for you to seem better than your friends and acquaintances. Now, to show there are not so many bigots as there used to be, there's a young man going to meet us at the station who is greatly interested in the study of social problems. He is going along with us just to look into this sort of thing and study it. It is impossible for him to understand people of our class, or do anything to make their condition better, if he does not thoroughly investigate their methods of life and action. He's going along just as a student, nothing more; and he may be down on the whole thing for all I know. He pays me five dollars for the privilege of accompanying me, and whether he likes it or not is his business. I want you to go along as a mechanic, and if your conscience won't let you take any share in the profit, I'll just pay you for your time.'

"'James Barlow,' said I, 'I am going with you, but for a purpose far different from that you desire. I shall keep by your side, and if I can dissuade you from committing the crime you intend I shall do so; but if I fail in this, and you deliberately break into a house for purposes of robbery, I shall arouse the inmates and frustrate your crime.' Now, James Barlow," said he, turning to the stout man with a severe expression on his strongly marked face, "is not what I have said perfectly true? Did you not say to me every word which I have just repeated?"

The stout man looked at the other in a very odd way. His face seemed to broaden and redden, and he merely closed his eyes as he promptly answered: —

"That's just what I said, every blasted word of it. You've told it fair and square, leavin' off nothin' and puttin' in nothin'. You've told the true facts out and out, up and down, without a break."

"Now, ladies," continued the tall man, "you see my story is corroborated, and I will conclude it by saying that when this house, in spite of my protest, had been opened, I entered with the others with the firm intention of stepping into a hallway or some other suitable place and announcing in a loud voice that the house was about to be robbed. As soon as I found the family aroused and my purpose accomplished, I intended to depart as quickly as possible, for, on account of the shadow cast upon me by my father's crime, I must never be found even in the vicinity of criminal action. But as I was passing through this room I could not resist the invitation of Barlow to partake of the refreshments which we saw upon the table. I was faint from fatigue and insufficient nourishment. It seemed a very little thing to taste a drop of wine in a house where I was about to confer a great benefit. I yielded to the temptation, and now I am punished. Partaking even that little which did not belong to me, I find myself placed in my present embarrassing position."

"You are right there," said I, "it must be embarrassing; but before we have any more reflections, there are some practical points about which I wish you would inform me. How did that wicked man, Mr. Barlow I think you called him, get into this house?"

The tall man looked at me for a moment, as if in doubt what he should say; and then his expression of mingled hopelessness and contrition changed into one of earnest frankness.

"I will tell you, sir, exactly," he said; "I have no wish to conceal anything. I have long wanted to have an opportunity to inform occupants of houses, especially those in the suburbs, of the insufficiency of their window fastenings. Familiar with mechanic devices as I am, and accustomed to think of such things, the precautions of householders sometimes move me to laughter. Your outer doors, front and back, are of heavy wood, chained, locked, and bolted, often double locked and bolted; but your lower windows are closed in the first place by the lightest kind of shutters, which are very seldom fastened at all, and in the second place by a little contrivance connecting the two sashes, which is held in place by a couple of baby screws. If these contrivances are of the best kind and cannot be opened from the outside with a knife-blade or piece of tin, the burglar puts a chisel or jimmy under the lower sash and gently presses it upward, when the baby screws come out as easily as if they were babies' milk-teeth. Not for a moment does the burglar trouble himself about the front door, with its locks and chains and bolts. He goes to the window, with its baby screws, which might as well be left open as shut, for all the hindrance it is to his entrance; and if he meddled with the door at all, it is simply to open it from the inside, so that when he is ready to depart he may do so easily."

"But all that does not apply to my windows," I said. "They are not fastened that way."

"No, sir," said the man, "your lower shutters are solid and strong as your doors. This is right, for if shutters are intended to obstruct entrance to a house they should be as strong as the doors. When James Barlow first reached this house he tried his jimmy on one of the shutters in this main building, but he could not open it. The heavy bolt inside was too strong for him. Then he tried another near by with the same result. You will find the shutters

splintered at the bottom. Then he walked
to the small addition at the back of the
house, where the kitchen is located. Here
the shutters were smaller, and of course
the inside bolts were smaller. Everything
in harmony. Builders are so careful now-
a-days to have everything in harmony.
When Barlow tried his jimmy on one of
these shutters the bolt resisted for a time,
but its harmonious proportions caused it
to bend, and it was soon drawn from its
staples and the shutter opened, and of
course the sash was opened as I told you
sashes are opened."

"Well," said I, "shutters and sashes of
mine shall never be opened in that way
again."

"It was with that object that I spoke to
you," said the tall man. "I wish you to
understand the faults of your fastenings,
and any information I can give you which
will better enable you to protect your
house, I shall be glad to give, as a slight
repayment for the injury I may have
helped to do to you in the way of broken
glass and spoiled carpet. I have made
window fastenings an especial study, and,
if you employ me for the purpose, I'll
guarantee that I will put your house into a

condition which will be absolutely burglar proof. If I do not do this to your satisfaction, I will not ask to be paid a cent."

"We will not consider that proposition now," I said, "for you may have other engagements which would interfere with the proposed job." I was about to say that I thought we had enough of this sort of story, when Aunt Martha interrupted me.

"It seems to me," she said, speaking to the tall burglar, "that you have instincts, and perhaps convictions, of what is right and proper; but it is plain that you allow yourself to be led and influenced by unprincipled companions. You should avoid even the outskirts of evil. You may not know that the proposed enterprise is a bad one, but you should not take part in it unless you know that it is a good one. In such cases you should be rigid."

The man turned toward my aunt, and looked steadfastly at her, and as he gazed his face grew sadder and sadder.

"Rigid," he repeated; "that is hard."

"Yes," I remarked, "that is one of the meanings of the word."

Paying no attention to me, he continued: —

"Madam," said he, with a deep pathos

in his voice, "no one can be better aware than I am that I have made many mistakes in the course of my life; but that quality on which I think I have reason to be satisfied with myself is my rigidity when I know a thing is wrong. There occurs to me now an instance in my career which will prove to you what I say.

"I knew a man by the name of Spotkirk, who had invented a liniment for the cure of boils. He made a great success with his liniment, which he called Boilene, and at the time I speak of he was a very rich man.

"One day Spotkirk came to me and told me he wanted me to do a piece of business for him, for which he would pay me twenty-five dollars. I was glad to hear this, for I was greatly in need of money, and I asked him what it was he wanted me to do.

"'You know Timothy Barker,' said he. 'Well, Timothy and I have had a misunderstanding, and I want you to be a referee or umpire between us, to set things straight.'

"'Very good,' said I, 'and what is the point of difference?'

"'I'll put the whole thing before you,'

said he, 'for of course you must understand it or you can't talk properly to Timothy. Now, you see, in the manufacture of my Boilene I need a great quantity of good yellow gravel, and Timothy Barker has got a gravel pit of that kind. Two years ago I agreed with Timothy that he should furnish me with all the gravel I should want for one-eighth of one per cent. of the profits on the Boilene. We didn't sign no papers, for which I am sorry, but that was the agreement; and now Timothy says that one-eighth of one per cent. isn't enough. He has gone wild about it, and actually wants ten per cent., and threatens to sue me if I don't give it to him.'

"'Are you obliged to have gravel? Wouldn't something else do for your purpose?'

"'There's nothing as cheap,' said Spotkirk. 'You see I have to have lots and lots of it. Every day I fill a great tank with the gravel and let water onto it. This soaks through the gravel, and comes out a little pipe in the bottom of the tank of a beautiful yellow color; sometimes it is too dark. and then I have to thin it with more water.'

" ' Then you bottle it,' I said.

" ' Yes,' said Spotkirk ; 'then there is all the expense and labour of bottling it.'

" ' Then you put nothing more into it,' said I.

" ' What more goes into it before it's corked,' said Spotkirk, ' is my business. That's my secret, and nobody's been able to find it out. People have had Boilene analyzed by chemists, but they can't find out the hidden secret of its virtue. There's one thing that everybody who has used it does know, and that is that it is a sure cure for boils. If applied for two or three days according to directions, and at the proper stage, the boil is sure to disappear. As a proof of its merit I have sold seven hundred and forty-eight thousand bottles this year.'

" ' At a dollar a bottle ? ' said I.

" ' That is the retail price,' said he.

" ' Now, then, Mr. Spotkirk,' said I, ' it will not be easy to convince Timothy Barker that one-eighth of one per cent. is enough for him. I suppose he hauls his gravel to your factory ? '

" ' Hauling's got nothing to do with it,' said he ; ' gravel is only ten cents a load anywhere, and if I choose I could put my factory right in the middle of a gravel pit. Timothy Barker has nothing to complain of.

"'But he knows you are making a lot of money,' said I, 'and it will be a hard job to talk him over. Mr. Spotkirk, it's worth every cent of fifty dollars.'

"'Now look here,' said he; 'if you get Barker to sign a paper that will suit me, I'll give you fifty dollars. I'd rather do that than have him bring a suit. If the matter comes up in the courts those rascally lawyers will be trying to find out what I put into my Boilene, and that sort of thing would be sure to hurt my business. It won't be so hard to get a hold on Barker if you go to work the right way. You can just let him understand that you know all about that robbery at Bonsall's clothing-store, where he kept the stolen goods in his barn, covered up with hay, for nearly a week. It would be a good thing for Timothy Barker to understand that somebody else beside me knows about that business, and if you bring it in right, it will fetch him around, sure.'

"I kept quiet for a minute or two, and then I said: —

" 'Mr. Spotkirk, this is an important business. I can't touch it under a hundred dollars.' He looked hard at me, and then he said : —

" ' Do it right, and a hundred dollars is yours.'

" After that I went to see Timothy Barker, and had a talk with him. Timothy was boiling over, and considered himself the worst-cheated man in the world. He had only lately found out how Spotkirk made his Boilene, and what a big sale he had for it, and he was determined to have more of the profits.

" ' Just look at it ! ' he shouted ; ' when Spotkirk has washed out my gravel it's worth more than it was before, and he sells it for twenty-five cents a load to put on gentlemen's places. Even out of that he makes a hundred and fifty per cent. profit.'

" I talked a good deal more with Timothy Barker, and found out a good many things about Spotkirk's dealings with him, and then in an off-hand manner I mentioned the matter of the stolen goods in his barn, just as if I had known all about it from the very first. At this Timothy stopped shouting, and became as meek as a mouse. He said nobody was as sorry as he was when he found the goods concealed in his barn had been stolen, and that if he had known it before the thieves took them away he should have informed the authorities; and then he went on to tell me how he got so poor and so hard up by giving his whole time to digging and hauling gravel for Spotkirk, and neglecting his little farm, that he did not know what was going to become of him and his family if he couldn't make better terms with Spotkirk for the future, and he asked me very earnestly to help him in this business if I could.

"Now, then, I set myself to work to consider this business. Here was a rich man oppressing a poor one, and here was this rich man offering me one hundred dollars — which in my eyes was a regular fortune — to help him get things so fixed that he could keep on oppressing the poor one. Now, then, here was a chance for me to show my principles. Here was a chance for me to show myself what you, madam, call rigid; and rigid I was. I just set that dazzling one hundred dollars aside, much as I wanted it. Much as I actually needed it, I wouldn't look at it, or think of it. I just said to myself, 'If you can do any

good in this matter, do it for the poor man;'
and I did do it for Timothy Barker with his
poor wife and seven children, only two of
them old enough to help him in the gravel
pit. I went to Spotkirk and I talked to
him, and I let him see that if Timothy
Barker showed up the Boilene business, as
he threatened to do, it would be a bad day
for the Spotkirk family. He tried hard to
talk me over to his side, but I was rigid,
madam, I was rigid, and the business
ended in my getting seven per cent. of the
profits of Boilene for that poor man, Timothy Barker, and his large family; and
their domestic prosperity is entirely due
— I say it without hesitation — to my
efforts on their behalf, and to my rigidity
in standing up for the poor against the
rich."

"Of course," I here remarked, "you
don't care to mention anything about the
money you squeezed out of Timothy Barker by means of your knowledge that he
had been a receiver of stolen goods, and I
suppose the Boilene man gave you something to get the percentage brought down
from ten per cent. to seven."

The tall burglar turned and looked at
me with an air of saddened resignation.

" Of course," said he, " it is of no use for a man in my position to endeavour to set himself right in the eyes of one who is prejudiced against him. My hope is that those present who are not prejudiced will give my statements the consideration they deserve."

" Which they certainly will do," I continued. Turning to my wife and Aunt Martha, " As you have heard this fine story, I think it is time for you to retire."

" I do not wish to retire," promptly returned Aunt Martha. " I was never more awake in my life, and couldn't go asleep if I tried. What we have heard may or may not be true, but it furnishes subjects for reflection — serious reflection. I wish very much to hear what that man in the middle of the bench has to say for himself; I am sure he has a story."

" Yes, ma'am," said the stout man, with animation, " I've got one, and I'd like nothin' better than to tell it to you if you'll give me a little somethin' to wet my lips with — a little beer, or whiskey and water, or anything you have convenient."

" Whiskey and water ! " said Aunt Martha with severity. " I should think not.

It seems to me you have had all the intoxicating liquors in this house that you would want."

"But I don't think you're the kind of person who'd doctor the liquor. This is the first gentleman's house where I ever found anything of that kind."

"The worse for the gentleman," I remarked. The man grunted.

"Well, ma'am," he said, "call it anything you please — milk, cider, or, if you have nothin' else, I'll take water. I can't talk without somethin' soaky."

My wife rose. "If we are to listen to another story," she said, "I want something to keep up my strength. I shall go into the dining-room and make some tea, and Aunt Martha can give these men some of that if she likes."

The ladies now left the room, followed by Alice. Presently they called me, and, leaving the burglars in charge of the vigilant David, I went to them. I found them making tea.

"I have been upstairs to see if George William is all right, and now I want you to tell me what you think of that man's story," said my wife.

"I don't think it a story at all," said I.

"I call it a lie. A story is a relation which purports to be fiction, no matter how much like truth it may be, and is intended to be received as fiction. A lie is a false statement made with the intention to deceive, and that is what I believe we have heard to-night."

"I agree with you exactly," said my wife.

"It may be," said Aunt Martha, "that the man's story is true. There are some things about it which make me think so; but if he is really a criminal he must have had trials and temptations which led him into his present mode of life. We should consider that."

"I have been studying him," I said, "and I think he is a born rascal, who ought to have been hung long ago."

My aunt looked at me. "John," she said, "if you believe people are born criminals, they ought to be executed in their infancy. It could be done painlessly by electricity, and society would be the gainer, although you lawyers would be the losers. But I do not believe in your doctrine. If the children of the poor were properly brought up and educated, fewer of them would grow to be criminals."

" I don't think this man suffered for want of education," said my wife; "he used very good language; that was one of the first things that led me to suspect him. It is not likely that sons of boat-builders speak so correctly and express themselves so well."

" Of course, I cannot alter your opin-ions," said Aunt Martha, " but the story interested me, and I very much wish to hear what that other man has to say for himself."

" Very well," said I, "you shall hear it; but I must drink my tea and go back to the prisoners."

" And I," said Aunt Martha, "will take some tea to them. They may be bad men, but they must not suffer."

I had been in the library but a few moments when Aunt Martha entered, fol-lowed by Alice, who bore a tray contain-ing three very large cups of tea and some biscuit.

" Now, then," said Aunt Martha to me, " if you will untie their hands, I will give them some tea."

At these words each burglar turned his eyes on me with a quick glance. I laughed.

"Hardly," said I. "I would not be willing to undertake the task of tying them up again, unless, indeed, they will consent to drink some more of my wine."

"Which we won't do," said the middle burglar, "and that's flat."

"Then they must drink this tea with their hands tied," said Aunt Martha, in a tone of reproachful resignation, and, taking a cup from the tray, she approached the stout man and held it up to his lips. At this act of extreme kindness we were all amused, even the burglar's companions smiled, and David so far forgot himself as to burst into a laugh, which, however, he quickly checked. The stout burglar, however, saw nothing to laugh at. He drank the tea, and never drew breath until the cup was emptied.

"I forgot," said my aunt, as she removed the cup from his lips, "to ask you whether you took much or little sugar."

"Don't make no difference to me," answered the man; "tea isn't malt liquor; it's poor stuff any way, and it doesn't matter to me whether it's got sugar in it or not, but it's moistenin', and that's what I want. Now, madam, I'll just say to you, if ever I break into a room where you're sleepin', I'll see that you don't come to no harm, even if you sit up in bed and holler."

"Thank you," said Aunt Martha; "but I hope you will never again be concerned in that sort of business."

He grinned. "That depends on circumstances," said he.

Aunt Martha now offered the tall man some tea, but he thanked her very respectfully, and declined. The young man also said that he did not care for tea, but that if the maid — looking at Alice — would give him a glass of water he would be obliged. This was the first time he had spoken. His voice was low and of a pleasing tone. David's face grew dark, and we could see that he objected to this service from Alice.

"I will give him the water myself," said Aunt Martha. This she did, and I noticed that the man's thirst was very soon satisfied. When David had been refreshed, and biscuits refused by the burglars, who could not very well eat them with their hands tied, we all sat down, and the stout man began his story. I give it as he told it, omitting some coarse and rough expressions, and a good deal of slang which would be unintelligible to the general reader.

"There's no use," said the burglar, "for me to try and make any of you believe that I'm a pious gentleman under a cloud, for I know I don't look like it, and wouldn't be likely to make out a case."

At this the tall man looked at him very severely.

"I don't mean to say," he continued, "that my friend here tried anything like that. Every word he said was perfectly true, as I could personally testify if I was called upon the stand, and what I'm goin' to tell you is likewise solid fact.

"My father was a cracksman, and a first-rate one, too; he brought me up to the business, beginning when I was very small. I don't remember havin' any mother, so I'll leave her out. My old man was very particular; he liked to see things done right. One day I was with him, and we saw a tinner nailing a new leader or tin water-spout to the side of a house.

"'Look here, young man,' says Dad, 'you're makin' a pretty poor job of that. You don't put in enough nails, and they ain't half drove in. Supposin' there was a fire in that house some night, and the family had to come down by the spout, and your nails would give way, and they'd break their necks. What would you think then? And I can tell you what it is, young man, I can appear ag'in you for doing poor work.'

" The tinner grumbled, but he used more nails and drove 'em tight, Dad and me standin' by, an' looking at him. One rainy night not long after this Dad took me out with him and we stopped in front of this house. 'Now, Bobbie,' said he, 'I want you to climb into that open second-story window, and then slip down stairs and open the front door for me; the family's at dinner.'

"'How am I to get up, Dad?' said I.

"'Oh, you can go up the spout,' says he; 'I'll warrant that it will hold you. I've seen to it that it was put on good and strong.'

" I tried it, and as far as I can remember I never went up a safer spout."

"And you opened the front door?" asked Aunt Martha.

"Indeed I did, ma'am," said the burglar, "you wouldn't catch me makin' no mistakes in that line.

"After a while I got too heavy to climb spouts, and I took to the regular business, and did well at it, too."

"Do you mean to say," asked Aunt Martha, "that you willingly and premeditatedly became a thief and midnight robber?"

"That's what I am, ma'am," said he; "I don't make no bones about it. I'm a number one, double-extra, back-springed, copper-fastened burglar, with all the attachments and noiseless treadle. That's what I am, and no mistake. There's all kinds of businesses in this world, and there's got to be people to work at every one of 'em; and when a fellow takes any particular line, his business is to do it well; that's my motto. When I break into a house I make it a point to clean it out first-class, and not to carry away no trash, nuther. Of course, I've had my ups and my downs, like other people, — preachers and doctors and storekeepers, — they all have them, and I guess the downs are more amusin' than the ups, at least to outsiders. I've just happened to think of one of them, and I'll let you have it.

"There was a man I knew named Jerry

Hammond, that was a contractor, and sometimes he had pretty big jobs on hand, buildin' or road-makin' or somethin' or other. He'd contract to do anything, would Jerry, no matter whether he'd ever done it before or not. I got to know his times and seasons for collecting money, and I laid for him."

"Abominable meanness!" exclaimed my wife.

"It's all business," said the stout man, quite unabashed. "You don't catch a doctor refusin' to practise on a friend, or a lawyer, nuther, and in our line of business it's the same thing. It was about the end of October, nigh four years ago, that I found out that Jerry had a lot of money on hand. He'd been collectin' it from different parties, and had got home too late in the day to put it in the bank, so says I to myself, this is your time, old fellow, and you'd better make hay while the sun shines. I was a little afraid to crack Jerry's house by myself, for he's a strong old fellow, so I got a man named Putty Henderson to go along with me. Putty was a big fellow and very handy with a jimmy; but he was awful contrary-minded, and he wouldn't agree to clean

out Jerry until I promised to go halves
with him. This wasn't fair, for it wasn't
his job, and a quarter would have been
lots for him.

"But there wasn't no use arguin', and
along we went, and about one o'clock we
was standin' alongside Jerry's bed, where
he was fast asleep. He was a bachelor,
and lived pretty much by himself. I give
him a punch to waken him up, for we'd
made up our minds that that was the way
to work this job. It wouldn't pay us to
go around huntin' for Jerry's money. He
was such a sharp old fellow, it was six to
four we'd never find it. He sat up in bed
with a jump like a hop-toad, and looked
'rst at one and then at the other of us.
We both had masks on, and it wasn't puz-
zlin' to guess what we was there fur.

"'Jerry Hammond,' says I, speakin'
rather rough and husky, 'we knows that
you've got a lot o' money in this house,
and we've come fur it. We mean business, and there's no use foolin'. You can
give it to us quiet and easy, and keep a
whole head on your shoulders, or we'll lay
you out ready fur a wake and help ourselves to the funds; and now you pays
your money and you can take your choice

how you do it. There's nothin' shabby about us, but we mean business. Don't we, pard?'—'That's so,' says Putty.

"'Look here,' says Jerry, jest as cool as if he had been sittin' outside on his own curbstone, 'I know you two men and no mistake. You're Tommy Randall, and you're Putty Henderson, so you might as well take off them masks.'—'Which I am glad to do,' says I, 'for I hate 'em,' and I put mine in my pocket, and Putty he took off his."

"Excuse me," said Aunt Martha, interrupting at this point, "but when Mr. Hammond mentioned the name of Tommy Randall, to whom did he refer?"

"I can explain that, madam," said the tall burglar, quickly. "This man by his criminal course of life has got himself into a good many scrapes, and is frequently obliged to change his name. Since I accidentally became acquainted with him he has had several aliases, and I think that he very often forgets that his real name is James Barlow."

"That's so," said the stout man, "there never was a more correct person than this industrious and unfortunate man sittin' by me. I am dreadful forgetful, and sometimes I disremember what belongs to me and what don't. Names the same as other things.

"'Well, now, Jerry,' says I, 'you needn't think you're goin' to make anythin' by knowin' us. You've got to fork over your cash all the same, and if you think to make anything by peachin' on us after we've cleared out and left you peaceful in your bed, you're mistook so far as I'm concerned; for I've made the track clear to get out of this town before daybreak, and I don't know when I'll come back. This place is gettin' a little too hot for me, and you're my concludin' exercise.' Jerry he sat still for a minute, considerin'. He wasn't no fool, and he knowed that there wasn't no use gettin' scared, nor cussin', nor hollerin'. What's more, he knowed that we was there to get his money, and if he didn't fork it over he'd get himself laid out, and that was worse than losin' money any day. 'Now, boys,' says he, 'I'll tell you what I'll do. I'll make you an offer; a fair and square offer. What money I've got I'll divide even with you, each of us takin' a third, and I'll try to make up what I lose out of my next contract. Now nothin' could be no squarer than that.' — 'How much money have you got, Jerry?' says I, 'that's the first thing to know.' — 'I've got thirty-one hundred dollars even,' says he, 'and that will be one thousand and thirty-three dollars and thirty-three cents apiece. I've got bills to pay to-morrow for lumber and bricks, and my third will pay 'em. If I don't I'll go to pieces. You don't want to see me break up business, do you?' — 'Now, Jerry,' says I, 'that won't do. You haven't got enough to divide into three parts. Putty and me agree to go halves with what we get out of you, and when I lay out a piece of business I don't make no changes. Half of that money is for me, and half is for Putty. So just hand it out, and don't let's have no more jabberin'.'

"Jerry he looked at me pretty hard, and then says he: 'You're about the close-fisted and meanest man I ever met with. Here I offer you a third part of my money, and all you've got to do is to take it and go away peaceable. I'd be willin' to bet two to one that it's more than you expected to get, and yet you are not satisfied; now, I'll be hanged if I'm going to do business with you.' — 'You can be hanged if you like,' says I, 'but you'll do the business all the same.' — 'No, I won't,' says he, and he turns to Putty Henderson. 'Now, Putty,' says he, 'you've got a pile more sense that this pal of yourn, and I'm goin' to see if I can't do business with you. Now, you and me together can lick this Tommy Randall just as easy as not, and if you'll help me do it I'll not only divide the money with you, but I'll give you fifty dollars extra, so that instead of fifteen hundred and fifty dollars — that's all he'd given you, if he didn't cheat you — you'll have sixteen hundred, and I'll have fifteen hundred instead of the thousand and thirty-three dollars which I would have had left if my first offer had been took. So, Putty, what do you say to that?' Now, Putty, he must have been a little sore with me on account of the arguments we'd had about dividin', and he was mighty glad besides to get the chance of makin' fifty dollars extry, and so he said it was all right, and he'd agree. Then I thought it was about time for me to take in some of my sail, and says I: 'Jerry, that's a pretty good joke, and you can take my hat as soon as I get a new one, but of course I don't mean to be hard on you, and if you really have bills to pay to-mor-

row I'll take a third, and Putty'll take
another, and we'll go away peaceful.' —
'No, you won't,' sings out Jerry, and with
that he jumps out of bed right at me, and
Putty Henderson he comes at me from the
other side, and, between the two, they
gave me the worst lickin' I ever got in my
born days, and then they dragged me down
stairs and kicked me out the front door,
and I had hardly time to pick myself up
before I saw a policeman about a block off,
and if he hadn't been a fat one he'd had
me sure. It wouldn't have been pleasant,
for I was a good deal wanted about that
time.

"So you see, ladies and gents, that it's
true what I said, — things don't always go
right in our line of business no more than
any other one."

"I think you were served exactly right,"
said Aunt Martha; "and I wonder such an
experience did not induce you to reform."

"It did, ma'am, it did," said the burglar.
"I made a vow that night that if ever
again I had to call in any one to help me
in business of that kind I wouldn't go
pards with him. I'd pay him so much for
the job, and I'd take the risks, and I've
stuck to it.

"But even that don't always work. Luck sometimes goes ag'in' a man, even when he's working by himself. I remember a thing of that kind that was beastly hard on me. A gentleman employed me to steal his daughter."

"What!" exclaimed my wife and Aunt Martha. "Steal his own daughter! What do you mean by that?"

"That's what it was," said the stout burglar; "no more nor less. I was recommended to the gent as a reliable party for that sort of thing, and I met him to talk it over, and then he told me just how the case stood. He and his wife were separated, and the daughter, about eleven years old, had been given to her by the court, and she put it into a boardin' school, and the gent he was goin' to Europe, and he wanted to get the little gal and take her with him. He tried to get her once, but it slipped up, and so there wasn't no good in his showin' hisself at the school any more, which was in the country, and he knowed that if he expected to get the gal he'd have to hire a professional to attend to it.

"Now, when I heard what he had to say, I put on the strictly pious, and, says I, 'that's a pretty bad thing you're askin' me to do, sir, to carry away a little gal from its lovin' mother, and more 'an that, to take it from a school where it's gettin' all the benefits of eddication.' — 'Eddication,' says he; 'that's all stuff. What eddication the gal gets at a school like that isn't worth a row of pins, and when they go away they don't know nothin' useful, nor even anything tip-top ornamental. All they've learned is the pianer and higher mathematics. As for anythin' useful, they're nowhere. There isn't one of them could bound New Jersey or tell you when Washington crossed the Delaware.' — 'That may be, sir,' says I, 'but them higher branches comes useful. If Washington really did cross the Delaware, your little gal could ask somebody when it was, but she couldn't ask 'em how the pianer was played, nor what the whole multiplication table came to added up. Them things she'd have to learn how to do for herself. I give you my word, sir, I couldn't take a little gal from a school, where she was gettin' a number one eddication, silver forks and towels extry.' The gent looked pretty glum, for he was to sail the next day, and if I didn't do the job for him he didn't know who

would, and he said that he was sorry to
see that I was goin' back on him after the
recommend I'd had, and I said that I
wouldn't go back on him if it wasn't for
my conscience. I was ready to do any
common piece of business, but this stealin'
away little gals from lovin' mothers was
a leetle too much for me. 'Well,' says
he, 'there ain't no time to be lost, and
how much more will satisfy your conscience?' When I said a hundred dollars,
we struck the bargain.

"Well, we cut and dried that business
pretty straight. I took a cab and went
out to the school, and the gent he got the
key of a house that was to let about three
miles from the school, and he was to stay
there and look at that empty house until
I brought him the gal, when he was to
pay me and take her away. I'd like to
have had more time, so that I could go
out and see how the land laid, but there
wasn't no more time, and I had to do the
best I could. The gent told me they all
went a walkin' every afternoon, and that
if I laid low that would be the best time
to get her, and I must just fetch her
along, no matter who hollered.

"I didn't know exactly how I was going to manage it, but I took along with me a big bag that was made for the conveyance of an extinct millionaire, but which had never been used, owin' to beforehand arrangements which had been made with the party's family.

"I left the cab behind a bit of woods, not far from the school, and then I laid low, and pretty soon I seed 'em all coming out, in a double line, with the teacher behind 'em, for a walk. I had a description of the little gal as was wanted, and as they come nearer I made her out easy. She was the only real light-haired one in the lot. I hid behind some bushes in the side of the road, and when they come up, and the light-haired little gal was just opposite to me, I jumped out of the bushes and made a dash at her. Whoop! what a row there was in one second! Such a screamin' and screechin' of gals, such a pilin' on top each other, and the teacher on top the whole of 'em, bangin' with her umbrella; they pulled at the gal and they pulled at me, an' they yelled and they howled, and I never was in such a row and hope I never shall be again, and I grabbed that girl by her frock, and I tumbled some over one way and some another, and I got the umbrella over my head, but I didn't mind it, and I clapped that bag over the little gal, and I jerked up her feet and let her slip into it, and then I took her up like a bag of meal, and put across the field, with the whole kit and boodle after me. But I guess most of 'em must have tumbled down in hysterics, judgin' from the screechin', and I got up to the cab and away we went. Well, when we got to the house where I was to meet the gent, he began straight off to blow at me. 'What do you mean,' he yelled, 'bringin' my daughter in a bag?' — 'It's the only way to do it, sir,' says I; 'they can't holler and they can't kick, and people passin' by don't know what you've got,' and so sayin' I untied the strings, put the little gal on her feet, and pulled off the bag, and then I'd be hanged if I ever saw a man so ragin' mad as he was. 'What do I want with that gal?' he cried; 'that's not my daughter. That girl's hair is as black as a coal, and she's a Jew besides.' As soon as I sot my eyes on the little varmint it come over me that I got the thing crooked, and in the scrimmage I let go of the right gal and grabbed another.

"I don't see how a man could help makin' mistakes with that school-teacher's umbrella whanging away at his knowledge box, but I wasn't goin' to let on. 'She ain't no Jew, nuther,' says I, 'and she's your daughter, too; you needn't try to play no tricks on me. Pay me my money and take her away as quick as you can, that's my advice, or before you know it you'll be nabbed.' — 'Pay ye!' he yelled; 'do you think I'd pay you anything for that little Jew?' — 'She's just as much a Christian as you are,' says I. 'Ain't you a Christian, little gal? and is'nt this gentleman your father? and ain't you surprised that he wants to give you back to be put in the bag?' I said this hopin' she'd have sense enough to say he was her father so's to get rid of me.

"The wretched gal had been clean dumbfounded when she was took out of the bag, and hadn't done nothin' so far but blubber and cry, and try to get away, which she couldn't, because I held her frock; but now she ups and screams he wasn't her father, and she'd never seen him before, and then he storms and swears, and tells me to take her back where I got her, and I tell him I'll see him hanged first, and what I want is my money; she screams, and he swears he'll not pay me a cent, and I squares off and says that I'll thrash him out of his skin, and then he calls in his coachman, and they both make at me, and I backs out the door to get my cabby to stand by me, and I found that he'd cut out, havin' most likely got frightened, afraid of bein' mixed up in trouble. Then I seed on the high road, some half a mile away, some men comin' gallopin', and the gent he looked out and seed 'em, too, and then says he to me, 'You'll jist take that little Jew gal back where you got her from; she's no use to me; I'm goin';' and at that I hollered for my money, and made a grab at him, but the coachman he tripped me over backward, and before I could git up again they was both off with the horses on a run.

"I was so mad I couldn't speak, but there wasn't no time for foolin', and I hadn't made up my mind which door I should cut out of, when the fellows on horseback went ridin' past as hard as they could go. They must have seed the carriage drivin' away, and thought for sure it had the gal in it, and they was after it, lickety-split.

"When they was clean gone I looked round for the little gal, but couldn't see her, but all a-sudden she came out of the fireplace, where she'd been hidin'. She'd got over her cryin', and over her scare, too, judgin' from her looks. 'I'm glad he's gone,' says she, 'and I'm mighty glad, too, that Mr. Haskins and them other men didn't see me.' — 'Who's they?' says I. — 'They's neighbors,' says she; 'if they knew I was here they'd took me back.' — 'Well, you little minx,' say I, 'isn't that what you want?' — 'No,' says she. 'I didn't want to go with that man, for I don't know him, and I hate him, but I don't want to go back to that school. I hate it worse than anything in the whole world. You haven't no idea what a horrid place it is. They just work you to death, and don't give you half enough to eat. My constitution won't stand it. I've told Pop that, and he thinks so too, but Marm, she don't believe in it, and my stayin' there is all her doin'. I've been wantin' to get away for ever so long, but I didn't want to be took off in a bag; but now that I'm out of that horrid hole I don't want to go back, and if you'll take me home to Pop, I know he won't let me go back, and he'll pay you real handsome besides.' — 'Who's your Pop?" says I. — 'He's Mr. Groppeltacker, of Groppeltacker & Mintz, corset findings, seven hundred and something or other, I forget the number now, Broadway. Oh, Pop does a lot of business, I tell you, and he's got lots of money. He sends corset findings to South America, and Paris, and Chicago, and Madagascar, and the uttermost parts of the earth. I've heard him say that often, and you needn't be afraid of his not bein' able to pay you. A lot more than that man would have paid you for his little gal, if you'd catched the right one. So if you take me to Pop, and get me there safe and sound, it will be an awful good speck for you.'

"Now, I begins to think to myself that perhaps there was somethin' in what that little Jew gal was sayin', and that I might make something out of the gal after all. I didn't count on gettin' a big pile out of old Groppeltacker, — it wasn't likely he was that kind of a man, — but whatever I did get would be clean profit, and I might as well try it on. He couldn't make no charge ag'in me fur bringin' him his daughter, if she asked me to do it; so says I to her, 'Now, if I take you home

to your Pop, will you promise on your
word an' honour, that you won't say nothin'
about my carryin' you off in a bag, and
say that you seed me walkin' along the
road and liked my looks, and told me you
were sufferin', and asked me to take
you home to your kind parents, where you
might be took proper care of; and that I
said I wasn't goin' that way, but I'd do it
out of pure Christian charity, and nothin'
more nor less, and here you was? And
then, of course, you can tell him he ought
to do the handsome thing by me.' — 'I'll
do that,' says she, 'and I tell how you
talked to me awful kind for more than
an hour, tryin' to keep me to stay at the
school, and it wasn't till I got down on my
knees and weeped that you agreed to take
me to my kind father.' — 'All right,' says
I, 'I might as well take you along, but
we'll have to go back by the railroad and
foot it, at least two miles, to the station,
and I don't know about walkin' across the
country with a little girl dressed as fine as
you are. I might get myself suspicioned.'
— 'That's so,' says she; 'we might meet
somebody that'd know me,' and then she
wriggled up her little forehead and began
to think. I never did see such a little gal

as sharp as that one was; needles was
nothin' to her. In about a minute she says,
'Where's that bag of yourn?' — 'Here
it is,' says I; and then she took it and
looked at it up and down, with her head
cocked on one side. 'If I'd somethin' to
cut that bag with,' says she, 'I could fix
myself up so that nobody'd know me,
don't care who it was.' — 'I don't want
that bag cut,' says I; 'it's an extry good
bag; it was made for a particular purpose,
and cost money.' — 'Pop will pay expenses,'
says she; 'how much did it cost?' — 'It
was four dollars cash,' said I. — 'They
cheated you like everything,' says she;
'you could get a bag like that any day for
a dollar and seventy-five cents. Will you
let it go at that?' — 'All right,' says I, for
I was tickled to see how sharp that little
Jew gal was, and ten to one I'd throwed
away the bag before we got to town; so
she pulled a little book out of her pocket
with a pencil stuck in it, and turnin' over
to a blank page she put down, 'Bag, one
dollar and seventy-five;' then she borrows
my big knife, and holdin' the top of the
bag up ag'in her belt, she made me stick a
pin in it about a hand's-breadth from the
floor; then she took the knife and cut the

bag clean across, me a-holdin' one side of
it; then she took the top end of that bag
and slipped it on her, over her head and
shoulders, and tied the drawin' strings in
it round her waist, and it hung around
her just like a skirt, nearly touchin' the
ground; then she split open the rest of
the bag, and made a kind of shawl out of
it, puttin' it into shape with a lot o' pins,
and pinnin' it on herself real clever. She
had lots of pins in her belt, and she told me
that she never passed a pin in that school
without pickin' it up, and that she had
four hundred and fifty-nine of them now
in her room, which she was mighty sorry
to leave behind, and that these she had
now was this day's pickin' up.

"When she got done workin' at herself
you couldn't see not a ribbon nor a hem of
 er fine clothes; it was all black skirt and
shawl, and she'd put up her sleeve, so that
when her arm stuck out it was bare. Then
she took all the ribbons and flowers off her
hat, and crumpled it up, and when she
tied it on what a guy she was. 'Now,'
says she, 'I can go barefoot.' — 'Which
you won't,' says I, 'for you'll get your feet
all cut, but you can muddy your shoes,'
which she did, I pumpin' on 'em, so that

the dust in the back yard would stick.
Then we starts off across the country, and,
upon my word, I was pretty nigh ashamed
to be seen walkin' with such a little scare-
crow. When I bought the tickets at the
station she asked me how much they was,
and put it down in her book. When we
got into the cars the people all looked hard
at her, and I reckon they thought some
kind of a home had been burnt down, and
this was one of the orphans that had been
saved. But they didn't say nothin', and she
fixed herself as comfortable as you please;
and before long a boy came through
the car with fruit in a basket, and then
says she to me, 'I want two apples.' The
boy had gone past us, but I got up and
followed him and bought her two apples.
'How much did you give for them?' says
she, when I come back. — 'They was two
for five cents,' says I. — 'Well,' says she,
'they do stick you dreadful. Two for
three cents is all papa or I pays for apples
like them,' and she took out her little book
and put down, 'Apples, three cents.' —
'Very well, miss,' says I, 'but if you want
any more refreshments you buy 'em yourself.' — 'I think I'd better,' says she, and
she went to work eatin' them two apples.

She hadn't more than got through with 'em when the boy came around ag'in. 'I want a banana,' says she; 'lend me five cents,' which I did, and she put down, 'Cash, five cents.' Then the boy come up, and says she, 'How much are your bananas?' — 'Five cents,' said he. — 'For two?' says she.— 'No,' says he, 'for one.'—'What do you take me for?' says she. 'I've bought bananas before. I'll give you three cents for that one,' pointin' to the biggest in the lot. — 'I can't do that,' said the boy, 'the price is five cents.' — 'I'd like a banana,' says she, 'but I don't pay more'n three cents; take it or leave it,' and with that the boy went on. 'Now,' says I, 'you've gouged yourself out of a banana.' — 'Not a bit of it,' says she; 'he'll be back;' and in two minutes he was back, and said she might have it for three cents. 'Have you got two coppers?' said she. 'Let me see 'em.' He said he had, and showed 'em to her, and she took 'em and the banana, and then give him five cents, and then she didn't give the change to me, but put it in her pocket. 'Now,' says she, 'if you'd buy things that way, you'd be rich in time.'

"When we got to the city we took the

elevated and went up town to Forty-eighth street, and then walked over to her father's house. It was a big one, on one of the cross streets. When we got there, she told me to wait a minute, and, lookin' around to see that nobody was comin', she slipped off the skirt and the cape she had made and rolled 'em up in a bundle. 'It don't matter about my hat and shoes,' says she, ' but they wouldn't know me in such duds.' Then, handin' me the bundle, she said, ' For twenty-five cents you can get that bag mended just as good as new, so you can take it, and it will save us a dollar and a half.' — ' No, you don't,' says I, for I'd had enough of her stinginess. ' I don't touch that bag ag'in, and I made up my mind that minute to charge the old man five dollars' worth. When the front door was opened, the servant gal looked as if she couldn't believe her eyes, but my young woman was as cool as you please, and she had me showed into a room off the hall, and then she went up-stairs.

" I sat a-waitin' a long time, which gave me a good chance to look around at things. The room was real handsome, and I took a peep at the window fastenin's and the lay of the doors, thinkin' the knowledge might come in handy some time. Right in front of me on a table was a little yellow mouse, and it struck me as I looked at it that that must be gold. I listened if anybody was comin', and then I picked it up to see if it really was. I thought I heard the door-bell ring just then, and shut it up in my hand quick, but nobody went to the door; and then I looked at the little mouse, and if it wasn't pure gold it was the best imitation ever I see, so I slipped it quietly in my pocket to look at it ag'in when I had time.

"Pretty soon old Groppeltacker come in, shut the door, and sot down. 'So you brought my daughter back,' says he. — 'Yes,' says I. — 'And you expect to be paid for it,' says he. — 'Yes,' says I, 'I do.' — 'How much do you ask for your services?' says he. Now, this was a sort of a staggerer, for I hadn't made up my mind how much I was goin' to ask; but there wasn't time for no more thinkin' about it, and so says I, plum, 'A hundred dollars, and there was some expenses besides.' — 'Well, well,' says he, 'that seems like a good deal, just for bringin' a little gal from school. It couldn't have took you more'n a couple of hours.' — 'I don't charge for time,' says I, 'it's for

the risks and· the science of the thing.
There's mighty few men in this town could
have brought your daughter home as neat
as I did.' — 'Well, well,' says he, rubbin'
his hands, ' I expect I'll have to pay for
the whole term of the school, whether she's
there or not, and the business will come
heavy on me. Don't you think sixty dollars would pay you?' Now, I know when
you deal with this sort of a man there's
always a good deal of difference splittin';
and so, says I, 'No, it won't. I might take
ninety dollars, but that's the very lowest
peg.' — 'The very lowest?' says he, gettin'
up and walkin' about a little; and then I
thought I heard the door-bell ring again,
and I was dreadful afraid somebody would
come and call off the old man before he
finished the bargain. 'Well,' says I, 'we'll
call it eighty-five and expenses, and there
I'll stop.'

"Groppeltacker, now he sot down ag'in
and looked hard at me. 'I didn't ask you
to bring my daughter back,' says he, speakin' gruff, and very different from the way
he spoke before, ' and what's more, I didn't
want her back, and what's more yet, I'm
not goin' to pay you a red cent.' — 'Now,
look a-here,' says I, mighty sharp, 'none

o' that, old man; fork over the money or I'll lay you out stiff as a poker, and help myself. I'm not a fellow to be fooled with, and there's nobody in this house can stop me.' Old Groppeltacker, he didn't turn a hair, but just sot there, and says he, 'Before you blow any more, suppose you take my little gold mouse out of your pocket and hand it to me.' I must say I was took back at this, but I spoke back, as bold as brass, and said I never seed his gold mouse. 'O, ho!' says he, 'what you didn't see was the electric button under the table cover which rung a bell when the mouse was picked up. That's what I call my mouse-trap.'

"At this I jist b'iled over. 'Now,' says I, 'just you hand out every cent you've got, and your watch, too; not another word.' And I jumped up and clapped my hand on my pistol in my hip-pocket, and just at that minute there was a click and the nippers were on me, and there was a big policeman with his hand on my shoulder. I couldn't speak, I was so b'ilin' and so dumbfounded both at once. Old Groppeltacker he just leaned back and he laughed. 'You came in,' he said to the cop, 'jest the second I rang, and as soft as a cat, and the

first thing that I want you to do is to take
that gold mouse out of his pocket, and I'll
be on hand whenever you let me know I'm
wanted.' The cop he took the gold mouse
out of my pocket, and says he, 'I know
this fellow, and if I'm not mistook, they'll
be more charges than yourn made ag'in
him.' There wasn't no chance to show
fight, so I didn't do it, but I says to old
Groppeltacker, 'There's my expenses,
you've got to pay them, anyway.'— 'All
right,' says he, 'jist you send in your bill
marked correct, by my daughter, and I'll
settle it,' and he laughed again, and the
cop he took me off. Well, ladies and gents,
that little piece of business, together with
some other old scores, took me to Sing Sing
for three years, and it tain't six months
since I got out, so you can see for your-
selves what hard times a fellow in my line
of business sometimes has."

"Well," said Aunt Martha, "I don't approve of the Groppeltacker sort of people,
but if there were more of that kind I believe there would be fewer of your kind.
That story shows you in such a bad light
that I believe it's true."

"Every word of it," said the man. "I
wish it wasn't."

And now I spoke. "Since you claim to be a truth-telling being," I said to the stout burglar, "suppose you tell me why you never attempted before to break into my house. Every considerable dwelling in this neighbourhood has been entered, and I have no doubt you are the men who committed all the burglaries."

"No, sir," said he; "not men, I am the man who did 'em all; but these two friends of mine was never with me before in a bit of business like this. 'Tain't in their line. I have had pals with me, but they was professionals. These ain't cracksmen, they don't know nothin' about it; but this one is handy at tools, and that's the reason I brung him along, but you see he kicked, and was goin' to give me away, and this young gentleman "—

"Never mind about that young gentleman," I said; "I have a certain curiosity to know why my house was not entered when the others were."

"Well," said he, "I don't mind tellin' yer how that was. It was on account of your baby. We don't like to crack a house where there's a pretty small baby that's liable to wake up and howl any minute, and rouse up the rest of the family.

There's no workin' in a house with comfort when there's such a young one about. I'll tell you what it is, all your burglar-alarms and your dogs ain't worth nuthin' alongside of a baby for guardin' a house. If a cracksman ain't careful the alarms will go off, and if he don't know how to manage dogs, the dogs will bark. But by George, sir, there ain't no providin' ag'in a baby. He'll howl any time, and nobody can tell when, so I waited till your baby was a little more settled in its ways and slept soundly, and then we come along, and here we are."

This statement very much surprised me, and did not elate me. Without saying so to any one, I had flattered myself that the burglars had heard of my precautions, and of my excellent stock of firearms, and perhaps had got a notion that I would be an intrepid man to deal with, and it was somewhat humiliating to find that it was our baby the burglars were afraid of, and not myself. My wife was amazed.

"Can it be possible," she said, "that these people know so much about our baby, and that George William has been protecting this house?"

"It makes my flesh creep," said Aunt

Martha. " Do you know everything about all of us ? "

" Wish I did, ma'am," said the stout burglar; " wish I'd known about that beastly liquor."

" Well, we've had enough of this," said I, rising; " and, my dear, you and Aunt Martha must be ready to go to bed, and David and I will keep guard over these fellows until morning."

At this instant the youngest burglar spoke. His face wore a very anxious expression.

" May I ask, sir," he said, " what you intend to do with me in the morning ? "

" I have already said," I answered, " that I shall then hand over all of you to the officers of justice of this country."

" But, sir," said the young man, " you will surely except me. I am not at all concerned in this matter, and it would be of the greatest possible injury to me to be mixed up in it, or to be mentioned in public reports as an associate of a criminal. I'm not acquainted with the gentleman at the other end of the bench, but I have every reason to believe from what he said to me that he intended to notify you if this James Barlow proceeded to any open act.

For myself, I beg you will allow me to state who and what I am, and to tell you by what a strange concatenation of circumstances I happen to find myself in my present position — one which, I assure you, causes me the greatest embarrassment and anxiety."

"We've had enough story-telling for one night," said I, "and you had better reserve your statement for the magistrate."

Here Aunt Martha put in her voice.

"That is not fair," she said, "two of them have been allowed to speak, and this one has just as much right to be heard as the others. What do you say, Cornelia?"

I hoped that my wife would put herself on my side, and would say that we had enough of this sort of thing; but female curiosity is an unknown quantity, and she unhesitatingly replied that she would like to hear the young man's story. I sat down in despair. It was useless to endeavour to withstand this yearning for personal information, — one of the curses, I may say, of our present civilization. The young man gave no time for change of opinion, but immediately began. His voice was rich and rather low, and his manner exceedingly pleasing and gentle.

"I wish to state in the first place," said he, "that I am a reporter for the press. In the exercise of my vocation I have frequently found myself in peculiar and unpleasant positions, but never before have I been in a situation so embarrassing, so humiliating, as this. In the course of my studies and experiences I have found that in literature and journalism, as well as in art, one can make a true picture only of what one has seen. Imagination is all very well, often grand and beautiful; but imaginative authors show us their inner selves and not our outer world; there is to-day a demand for the real, and it is a demand which will be satisfied with nothing but the truth. I have determined, as far as in me lies, to endeavour to supply this demand, and I have devoted myself to the study of Realism.

"With this end in view, I have made it a rule never to describe anything I have not personally seen and examined. If we would thoroughly understand and appreciate our fellow-beings we must know what they do and how they do it; otherwise we cannot give them credit for their virtues, or judge them properly for their faults. If I could prevent crime I would annihilate it, and when it ceased to exist the necessity for describing it would also cease. But it does exist. It is a powerful element in the life of the human race. Being known and acknowledged everywhere, it should be understood ; therefore it should be described. The grand reality of which we are a part can never be truly comprehended until we comprehend all its parts. But I will not philosophize. I have devoted myself to Realism, and in order to be a conscientious student I study it in all its branches. I am frequently called upon to write accounts of burglars and burglaries, and in order thoroughly to understand these people and their method of action I determined, as soon as the opportunity should offer itself, to accompany a burglarious expedition. My sole object was the acquisition of knowledge of the subject, — knowledge which to me would be valuable, and, I may say, essential. I engaged this man, James Barlow, to take me with him the first time he should have on hand an affair of this kind, and thus it is that you find me here to-night in this company. As I came here for the purpose of earnest and thorough investigation, I will frankly admit that I would

not have interfered with his processes,
but at the same time I would have seen
that no material injuries should result to
any members of this family."

" That was very kind of you," I said, at
which my wife looked at me somewhat re-
proachingly.

" If he really intended it," she remarked,
" and I do not see why that was not the
case, it was kind in him."

" As for me," said Aunt Martha, very
sympathetically, " I think that the study
of Realism may be carried a great deal
too far. I do not think that there is the
slightest necessity for people to know anything about burglars. If people keep talking and reading about diseases they will
get them, and if they keep talking and
reading about crimes they will find that
iniquity is catching, the same as some
other things. Besides, this realistic description gets to be very tiresome. If you
really want to be a writer, young man, why
don't you try your hand on some original
composition ? Then you might write
something which would be interesting."

" Ah, madam," said the young man, cast-
ing his eyes on the floor, " it would be far
beyond my power to write anything more

wonderful than what I have known and seen! If I may tell you some of the things which have happened to me, you will understand why I have become convinced that in this world of realities imagination must always take a second place."

"Of course we want to hear your story," said Aunt Martha; "that is what we are here for."

"If I was unbound," said the young man, looking at me, "I could speak more freely."

"No doubt of it," said I; "but perhaps you might run away before you finished your story. I wouldn't have that happen for the world."

"Don't make fun of him," said Aunt Martha. "I was going to ask you to cut him loose, but after what you say I think it would perhaps be just as well to keep them all tied until the narratives are completed."

With a sigh of resignation the young man began his story.

"I am American born, but my father, who was a civil engineer and of high rank in his profession, was obliged, when I was quite a small boy, to go to Austria, where

he had made extensive contracts for the
building of railroads. In that country I
spent the greater part of my boyhood and
youth. There I was educated in the best
schools, my father sparing no money to
have me taught everything that a gentleman should know. My mother died when
I was a mere infant, and as my father's
vocation made it necessary for him to
travel a great deal, my life was often a
lonely one. For society I depended entirely upon my fellow-scholars, my tutors,
and masters. It was my father's intention, however, that when I had finished
my studies I should go to one of the great
capitals, there to mix with the world.

"But when this period arrived I was
in no haste to avail myself of the advan-
tages he offered me. My tastes were
studious, my disposition contemplative,
and I was a lover of rural life.

"My father had leased an old castle in
Carinthia, not far from the mountains,
and here he kept his books and charts,
and here he came for recreation and study
whenever his arduous duties gave him a
little breathing-spell. For several months
I had lived at this castle, happy when my
father was with me and happy when I

was alone. I expected soon to go to Vienna, where my father would introduce me to some of his influential friends. But day by day I postponed the journey.

"Walking one morning a few miles from the castle, I saw at the edge of a piece of woodland a female figure seated beneath a tree. Approaching nearer, I perceived that she was young, and that she was sketching. I was surprised, for I knew that in this part of the world young women, at least those of the upper classes, to which the costume and tastes of this one showed her to belong, were not allowed to wander about the country by themselves; but although I stood still and watched the young lady for some time, no companion appeared upon the scene.

"The path I had intended to take led past the piece of woodland, and I saw no reason why I should diverge from my proposed course. I accordingly proceeded, and when I reached the young lady I bowed and raised my hat. I think that for some time she had perceived my approach, and she looked up at me with a face that was half merry, half inquisitive, and perfectly charming. I cannot describe the effect which her expression had upon

me. I had never seen her before, but her
look was not such a one as she would
bestow upon a stranger. I had the most
powerful desire to stop and speak to her,
but having no right to do so, I should
have passed on, had she not said to me,
in the best of English, ' Good-morning,
sir.' Then I stopped, you may be sure.
I was so accustomed to speak to those I
meet in either French or German that I
involuntarily said to her, ' *Bon jour, Mad-
emoiselle.*'—' You need not speak French,'
she said; ' I am neither English nor American, but I speak English. Are you the
gentleman who lives in Wulrick Castle?
If so, we are neighbours, and I wish you
would tell me why you live there all the
time alone.'

"At this I sat down by her. 'I am
that person,' I said, and handed her my
card. 'But before I say any more, please
tell me who you are.' — 'I am Marie Dor-
fler. My father's house is on the other
side of this piece of woodland; you cannot
see it from here; this is part of his estate.
And now tell me why you live all by
yourself in that old ruin.' — 'It is not
altogether a ruin,' I answered; 'part of it
is in very good condition.' And then I

proceeded to give her an account of my
method of life and my reasons for it. 'It
is interesting,' she said, 'but it is very
odd.' — 'I do not think it half so odd,' I
answered, ' as that you should be here by
yourself.' — 'That is truly an out-of-the-
way sort of thing,' she said ; 'but just now
I am doing out-of-the-way things. If I do
not do them now, I shall never have the
opportunity again. In two weeks I shall
be married, and then I shall go to Prague,
and everything will be by line and rule.
No more delightful rambles by myself.
No more sitting quietly in the woods
watching the little birds and hares. No
more making a sketch just where I please,
no matter whether the ground be damp
or not.' — ' I wonder that you are allowed
to do these things now,' I said. — 'I am
not allowed,' she answered. 'I do them
in hours when I am supposed to be paint-
ing flower pieces in an upper room.' — 'But
when you're married,' I said, 'your hus-
band will be your companion in such
rambles.' — 'Hardly,' she said, shrugging
her shoulders ; 'he will be forty-seven on
the thirteenth of next month, which I
believe is July, and he is a great deal more
grizzled than my father, who is past fifty.

He is very particular about all sorts of
things, as I suppose he has to be, as he is
a Colonel of infantry. Nobody could possibly disapprove of my present perform-
ances more than he would.' I could not
help ejaculating, 'Why, then, do you
marry him?' She smiled at my earnest-
ness. 'Oh, that is all arranged,' she said,
' and I have nothing to do with it. I have
known for more than a year that I'm to
marry Colonel Kaldhein, but I cannot say
that I have given myself much concern
about it until recently. It now occurs to
me that if I expect to amuse myself in the
way I best like I must lose no time doing so.'
I looked at the girl with earnest interest.
'It appears to me,' said I, 'that your ways
of amusing yourself are very much like
mine.' — 'That is true,' she said, looking
up with animation, 'they are. Is it not
delightful to be free, to go where you like,
and do what you please, without any one
to advise or interfere with you?' — 'It is
delightful,' said I; and for half an hour we
sat and talked about these delights and
kindred subjects. She was much interested in our castle, and urged me to make
a sketch of it, so that she may know what
it now looked like. She had seen it when

a little girl, but never since, and had been afraid to wander very far in this direction by herself. I told her that it would be far better for her to see the castle with her own eyes, and that I could conduct her to an eminence, not half a mile away, where she could have an excellent view of it. This plan greatly pleased her; but looking at her watch she said that it would be too late for her to go that morning, but if I happened to come that way the next day, and she should be there to finish her sketch, she would be delighted to have me show her the eminence."

"I think," interrupted Aunt Martha, "that she was a very imprudent young woman."

"That may be," he replied, "but you must remember, madam, that up to this time the young lady had been subjected to the most conventional trammels, and that her young nature had just burst out into temporary freedom and true life. It was the caged bird's flight into the bright summer air."

"Just the kind of birds," said Aunt Martha, "that shouldn't be allowed to fly, at least until they are used to it. But you can go on with your story."

"Well," said the young man, "the next day we met I took her to the piece of high ground I had mentioned, and she sketched the castle. After that we met again and again, nearly every day. This sort of story tells itself. I became madly in love with her, and I am sure she liked me very well; at all events I was a companion of her own age and tastes, and such a one, she assured me, she had never known before, and probably would never know again."

"There was some excuse for her," said Aunt Martha; "but still she had no right to act in that way, especially as she was so soon to be married."

"I do not think that she reasoned much upon the subject," said the young man, "and I am sure I did not. We made no plans. Every day we thought only of what we were doing or saying, and not at all what we had done or would do. We were very happy.

"One morning I was sitting by Marie in the very place where I had first met her, when we heard some one rapidly approaching. Looking up I saw a tall man in military uniform. 'Heavens!' cried Marie, 'it is Colonel Kaldhein.'

" The situation was one of which an expectant bridegroom would not be likely to ask many questions. Marie was seated on a low stone with her drawing-block in her lap. She was finishing the sketch on which she was engaged when I first saw her, and I was kneeling close to her, looking over her work and making various suggestions, and I think my countenance must have indicated that I found it very pleasant to make suggestions in that way to such a pretty girl. Our heads were very close together. Sometimes we looked at the paper, sometimes we looked at each other. But in the instant I caught sight of the Colonel the situation had changed. I rose to my feet, and Marie began to pick up the drawing materials, which were lying about her.

"Colonel Kaldhein came forward almost at a run. His eyes blazed through his gold spectacles, and his close-cut reddish beard seemed to be singeing with the fires of rage. I had but an instant for observation, for he came directly up to me, and with a tremendous objurgation he struck me full in the face with such force that the blow stretched me upon the ground.

" I was almost stunned ; but I heard

a scream from Marie, a storm of angry words from Kaldhein, and I felt sure he was about to inflict further injury. He was a much stronger man than I was, and probably was armed. With a sudden instinct of self-preservation I rolled down a little declivity on the edge of which I had fallen, and staggering to my feet, plunged into a thicket and fled. Even had I been in the full possession of my senses, I knew that under the circumstances I would have been of no benefit to Marie had I remained upon the scene. The last thing I heard was a shout from Kaldhein, in which he declared that he would kill me yet. For some days I did not go out of my castle. My face was bruised, my soul was dejected. I knew there was no possible chance that I should meet Marie, and that there was a chance that I might meet the angry Colonel. An altercation at this time would be very annoying and painful to the lady, no matter what the result, and I considered it my duty to do everything that was possible to avoid a meeting with Kaldhein. Therefore, as I have said, I shut myself up within the walls of old Wulrick, and gave strict orders to my servants to admit no one.

"It was at this time that the strangest events of my life occurred. Sitting in an upper room, gazing out of the window, over the fields, through which I had walked so happily but two days before to meet the lady whom I had begun to think of as my Marie, I felt the head of a dog laid gently in my lap. Without turning my head I caressed the animal, and stroked the long hair on his neck.

"My hound Ajax was a dear companion to me in this old castle, although I never took him in my walks, as he was apt to get into mischief, and when I turned my head to look at him he was gone; but strange to say, the hand which had been stroking the dog felt as if it were still resting on his neck.

"Quickly drawing my hand toward me it struck the head of the dog, and, moving it backward and forward, I felt the ears and nose of the animal, and then became conscious that its head was still resting upon my knee.

"I started back. Had I been stricken with blindness? But no; turning my head, I could plainly see everything in the room. The scene from the window was as distinct as it ever had been. I sprang to my feet, and, as I stood wondering what this strange thing could mean, the dog brushed up against me and licked my hand. Then the idea suddenly flashed into my mind that by some occult influence Ajax had been rendered invisible.

"I dashed down-stairs, and although I could neither see nor hear it, I felt that the dog was following me. Rushing into the open air, I saw one of my men. 'Where is Ajax?' I cried. 'A very strange thing has happened, sir,' he said, 'and I should have come to tell you of it, had I not been unwilling to disturb your studies. About two hours ago Ajax was lying here in the courtyard; suddenly he sprang to his feet with a savage growl. His hair stood straight upon his back, his tail was stiff, and his lips were drawn back, showing his great teeth. I turned to see what had enraged him, but there was absolutely nothing, sir, — nothing in the world. And never did I see Ajax so angry. But this lasted only for an instant. Ajax suddenly backed, his tail dropped between his legs, his head hung down, and with a dreadful howl he turned, and, leaping the wall of the courtyard, he disappeared. I have since been watch-

ing for his return. The gate is open, and
as soon as he enters I shall chain him, for
I fear the dog is mad.'

"I did not dare to utter the thoughts
that were in my mind, but, bidding the
man inform me the moment Ajax returned, I reëntered the castle and sat
down in the great hall.

"The dog was beside me; his head
again lay upon my knees. With a feeling
of awe, yet strangely enough without fear,
I carefully passed my hand over the animal's head. I felt his ears, his nose, his
jaws, and his neck. They were not the
head, the ears, the nose, the jaws, or the
neck of Ajax!

"I had heard of animals, and even human
beings, who were totally invisible, but who
still retained their form, their palpability,
and all the powers and functions of life. I
had heard of houses haunted by invisible
animals; I had read De Kay's story of
the maiden Manmat'ha, whose coming her
lover perceived by the parting of the tall
grain in the field of ripe wheat through
which she passed, but whose form, although
it might be folded in his arms, was yet as
invisible to his sight as the summer air.
I did not doubt for a moment that the ani-

mal that had come to me was one of those strange beings. I lifted his head; it was heavy. I took hold of a paw which he readily gave me; he had every attribute of a real dog, except that he could not be seen."

" I call that perfectly horrible," said Aunt Martha with a sort of a gasp.

" Perhaps," said the young man, " you would prefer that I should not continue."

At this both my wife and Aunt Martha declared that he must go on, and even I did not object to hearing the rest of the story.

" Well," said the young man, " Ajax never came back. It is generally believed that dogs can see things which are invisible to us, and I am afraid that my faithful hound was frightened, perhaps to death, when he found that the animal whose entrance into the courtyard he had perceived was a supernatural thing.

" But if I needed a canine companion I had one, for by day or night this invisible dog never left me. When I slept he lay on the floor by the side of my bed; if I put down my hand I could always feel his head, and often he would stand up and press his nose against me, as if to assure me that he was there. This strange companionship continued for several days, and I became really attached to the invisible animal. His constant companionship seemed to indicate that he had come to guard me, and that he was determined to do it thoroughly. I felt so much confidence in his protection, although I knew not how it could be exerted, that one morning I decided to take a walk, and with my hand on the head of the dog, to make sure that he was with me, I strolled into the open country.

"I had walked about a mile, and was approaching a group of large trees, when suddenly from behind one of them the tall figure of a man appeared. In an instant I knew it to be Colonel Kaldhein; his was a face which could not easily be forgotten. Without a word he raised a pistol which he held in his hand and fired at me. The ball whistled over my head.

"I stopped short, startled, and frightened almost out of my senses. I was unarmed, and had no place of refuge. It was plain that the man was determined to kill me.

"Quickly recocking his pistol, Kaldhein raised it again. I involuntarily shrank back, expecting death; but before he could fire his arm suddenly dropped, and the pistol was discharged into the ground. Then began a strange scene. The man shouted, kicked, and beat up and down with his arms; his pistol fell from his hand, he sprang from side to side, he turned around, he struggled and yelled.

"I stood astounded. For an instant I supposed the man had been overtaken by some sort of fit; but in a flash the truth came to me,—Kaldhein was being attacked by my protector, the invisible dog.

"Horrified by this conviction, my first impulse was to save the man; and, without knowing what I was going to do, I stepped quickly toward him, but stumbling over something I did not see I fell sprawling. Before I could regain my feet I saw Kaldhein fall backward to the ground, where a scene took place, so terrible that I shall not attempt to describe it. When, with trembling steps, I approached, the man was dead. The invisible dog had almost torn him to pieces.

"I could do nothing. I did not remain upon the spot another minute, but hurried home to the castle. As I rapidly walked on I felt the dog beside me, and, putting my hand upon him, I felt that he was panting terribly. For three days I did not leave the house.

"About the end of this time I was sitting in an upper room of the castle, reflecting upon the recent dreadful event, when the thought struck me that the invisible dog, who was by my side, apparently asleep, must be of an unusually powerful build to overcome so easily such a strong man as Kaldhein. I felt a desire to know how large the creature really was, and, as I had never touched any portion of his body back of his shoulders, I now passed my hand along his back. I was amazed at his length, and when I had moved my hand at least seven feet from his head it still rested upon his body. And then the form of that body began to change in a manner which terrified me ; but impelled by a horrible but irresistible curiosity, my hand moved on.

"But I no longer touched the body of a dog ; the form beneath my hand was cylindrical, apparently about a foot in diameter. As my hand moved on the diameter diminished, and the skin of the creature became cold and clammy. I was feeling the body of a snake !

" I now had reached the open door of the room. The body of the snake extended through it. It went on to the top of the stairs; these I began to descend, my heart beating fast with terror, my face blanched, I am sure, but my hand still moving along the body of the awful creature. I had studied zoölogy, giving a good deal of attention to reptiles, and I knew that, judged by the ordinary ratio of diminution of the bodies of serpents, this one must extend a long distance down the stairs.

" But I had not descended more than a dozen steps before I felt a shiver beneath my hand, and then a jerk, and the next moment the snake's body was violently drawn upward. I withdrew my hand and started to one side, and then, how, I know not, I became aware that the dog part of the creature was coming downstairs.

" I now became possessed by a wild terror. The creature must be furious that I had discovered his real form. He had always been careful to keep his head toward me. I should be torn to pieces as Kaldhein had been! Down the stairs I dashed, across the courtyard, and toward

a lofty old tower, which stood in one
corner of the castle. I ran up the wind-
ing stairs of this with a speed which
belongs only to a frantically terrified
creature, until I reached the fourth story,
where I dashed through an open doorway,
slammed behind me an iron door, which
shut with a spring, and fell gasping upon
the floor.

" In less than a minute I was aware,
by a slight rattling of the grate-hinges,
that something was pushing against the
door; but I did not move. I knew that I
was safe. The room in which I lay was a
prison dungeon, and in it, in the olden
times, it is said, men had been left to
perish. Escape or communication with
the outer world was impossible. A little
light and air came through a narrow slit in
the wall, and the door could not be forced.

" I knew that the invisible dog, or
whatever it was, could not get in unless
the door was open. I had frequently
noticed that when he entered a room it
was through an open door, and I sometimes knew of his approach by seeing
an unlatched door open without visible
cause ; so, feeling secure for the present,
I lay and gasped and panted.

"After the lapse of a few hours, however, I was seized by a new terror. How was I ever to get out of this horrible dungeon? Even if I made up my mind to face the dog, trusting that he had recovered from his momentary anger, I had no means of opening the door, and as to making any one hear me I knew that was impossible.

"I had no hope that my servants would seek me here. I had not seen any one when I ran into the tower, and if they should discover that I was in this dungeon, how could they open the door? The key was in my father's possession. He had taken it to Vienna to exhibit it as a curiosity to some of his mechanical friends. He believed that there was not such another key in the world. I was in the habit of making long absences from the castle, and if I should be looked for I believed that the tower would be the last place visited.

"Night came on; the little light in the room vanished, and, hungry, thirsty, and almost hopeless, I fell asleep.

"During the night there was a most dreadful storm. The thunder roared, the lightning flashed through the slit in the wall, and the wind blew with such terrific violence that the tower shook and trembled. After a time I heard a tremendous crash as of falling walls, and then another, and now I felt the wind blowing into my prison.

"There was no further sleep for me. Trembling with a fearful apprehension of what might happen next, I cowered against the wall until the day broke, and then I perceived that in front of me was a great hole in the wall of the dungeon, which extended for more than a yard above the floor. I sat and gazed at this until the light became stronger, and then I cautiously approached the aperture and looked out. Nearly the whole of the castle lay in ruins before me !

"It was easy to see what had happened. The storm had demolished the crumbling walls of the old building, and the tower, itself frail and tottering, stood alone, high above the prostrate ruins. If the winds should again arise it must fall, and at any moment its shaken foundations might give way beneath it.

"Through the hole in the wall, which had been caused by the tearing away of some of the connection between the tower

and main building, I could look down on
the ground below, covered with masses of
jagged stone; but there was no way in
which I could get down. I could not
descend that perpendicular wall. If I
leaped out, death would be certain.

" As I crouched at the opening I felt the
head of a dog pushed against me. A
spasm of terror ran through me, but the
moment the creature began to lick my
hands I knew that I had nothing to fear
from him. Instantly my courage returned.
I felt that he was my protector. I patted
his head and he renewed his caresses.

" Passing my hand over him, I found he
was holding himself in his present position
by means of his forelegs, which were
stretched out upon the floor. What a dog
this must be, who could climb a wall! But
I gave no time to conjectures of this sort.
How could I avail myself of his assistance?
In what manner could he enable me to escape from that dangerous tower?

" Suddenly a thought came to me. I
remembered the snake part of him. Judg-
ing from the ratio of diminution, which I
have mentioned before, that part, if hanging down, must reach nearly, if not quite,
to the ground. By taking advantage of

this means of descent I might be saved, but the feat would require dexterity and an immense amount of faith. This serpent-like portion of the animal was invisible. How could I know how long it was!

"But there was no time for consideration; the wind had again arisen, and was blowing with fury. The tower shook beneath me; at any moment it might fall. If I should again escape from death, through the assistance of my invisible friend, I must avail myself of that assistance instantly.

"I stopped and felt the animal. He still hung by part of his body and by his forelegs to the floor of the dungeon, and by reaching out I could feel that the rest of him extended downward. I therefore seized his body in my arms, threw myself out of the aperture, and began to slide down.

"In a very short time I found that I had reached the snake portion of the creature, and, throwing my arms and legs around it, I endeavoured with all my strength to prevent a too rapid descent; but in spite of all my efforts, my downward progress was faster than I would have wished it to be. But there was no stopping; I must slip down.

" In these moments of rapid descent my mind was filled with wild anxiety concerning the serpent-like form to which I was clinging. I remembered in a flash that there were snakes whose caudal extremity dwindled away suddenly into a point. This one might do so, and at any instant I might come to the end of the tail and drop upon the jagged stones below.

" Calculation after calculation of the ratio of diminution flashed through my mind during that awful descent. My whole soul was centred upon one point. When would this support end? When would I drop?

" Fortunately I was on the leeward side of the tower, and I was not swung about by the wind. Steadily I descended, and steadily the diameter of the form I grasped diminished; soon I could grasp it in my hand; then with a terrified glance I looked below. I was still at a sickening distance from the ground. I shut my eyes. I slipped down, down, down. The tail became like a thick rope which I encircled with each hand. It became thinner and thinner. It grew so small that I could not hold it; but as I felt it slip from my fingers my feet rested on a pile of stones.

" Bewildered and almost exhausted, I stumbled over the ruins, gained the unencumbered ground, and ran as far from the tower as I could, sinking down at last against the trunk of a tree in a neighbouring field. Scarcely had I reached this spot when the fury of the wind-storm appeared to redouble, and before the wild and shrieking blast the tower bent and then fell with a crash upon the other ruins.

" The first thought that came into my mind when I beheld the dreadful spectacle concerned the creature who had twice saved my life. Had he escaped, or was he crushed beneath that mass of stone ? I felt on either side to discover if he were near me, but he was not. Had he given his life for mine ?

" Had I been stronger I would have searched for him ; I would have clambered among the ruins to see if I could discover his mangled form. If I could but reach his faithful head I would stroke and caress it, living or dead. But excitement, fatigue, and want of food had made me so weak that I could do nothing but sit upon the ground with my back against the tree.

" While thus resting I perceived that

the whole of the tower had not been demolished by the storm. Some of the rooms in which we had lived, having been built at a later date than the rest of the great edifice, had resisted the power of the wind and were still standing.

" From the direction of the uninjured portion of the castle I now saw approaching a light-coloured object, which seemed to be floating in the air about a foot from the ground. As it came nearer I saw that it was a basket, and I immediately understood the situation. My faithful friend was alive, and was bringing me some refreshments.

" On came the basket, rising and falling with the bounds of the dog. It was truly an odd spectacle, but a very welcome one. In a few moments the basket was deposited at my side, and I was caressing the head of the faithful dog. In the basket I found a bottle of wine and some bread and meat, which the good creature had doubtless discovered in the kitchen of the castle, and it was not long before I was myself again. The storm had now almost passed away, and I arose and went to my own rooms, my friend and protector still keeping close to my side.

" On the morning of the next day, as I sat wondering what had happened to my servants, and whether my father had been apprised of the disaster to the castle, I felt something pulling at the skirt of my coat. I put out my hand and found that it was the invisible dog. Imagining that he wished me to follow him, I arose, and, obeying the impulse given me by his gentle strain upon my coat, I followed him out of the door, across the courtyard, and into the open country. We went on for a considerable distance. A gentle touch of my coat admonished me when I turned from the direction in which it was desired that I should go.

" After a walk of about half an hour I approached a great 'oak-tree, with low, wide-spreading branches. Some one was sitting beneath it. Imagining the truth, I rushed forward. It was Marie!

" It was needless for us to say anything, to explain the state of our feelings toward each other. That tale was told by the delight with which we met. When I asked her how she came to be there, she told me that about an hour before, while sitting in front of her father's mansion, she had felt something gently pulling at her skirts;

and, although at first frightened, she was at length impelled to obey the impulse, and, without knowing whether it was the wind or some supernatural force which had led her here, she had come.

"We had a great deal to say to each other. She told me that she had been longing to send me a message to warn me that Colonel Kaldhein would certainly kill me the next time he saw me; but she had no means of sending me such a message, for the Colonel had had her actions closely watched.

"When the news came of Kaldhein's death she at first feared that I had killed him, and would therefore be obliged to fly the country; but when it was known that he had been almost torn to pieces by wild beasts, she, like every one else, was utterly amazed, and could not understand the matter at all. None but the most ferocious creatures could have inflicted the injuries of which the man had died, and where those creatures came from no one knew. Some people thought that a pack of blood-hounds might have broken loose from some of the estates of the surrounding country, and, in the course of their wild journeyings, might have met with the Colonel, and fallen upon him. Others surmised that a bear had come down from the mountains; but the fact was that nobody knew anything about it.

"I did not attempt to acquaint Marie with the truth. At that moment the invisible dog was lying at my side, and I feared if I mentioned his existence to Marie she might fly in terror. To me there was only one important phase of the affair, and that was that Marie was now free, that she might be mine.

"Before we parted we were affianced lovers, pledged to marry as soon as possible. I wrote to my father, asking for his permission to wed the lady. But in his reply he utterly forbade any such marriage. Marie also discovered that her parents would not permit a union with a foreigner, and would indeed oppose her marriage with any one at this time.

"However, as usual, love triumphed, and after surmounting many difficulties we were married and fled to America. Since that time I have been obliged to support myself and my wife, for my father will give me no assistance. He had proposed a very different career for me, and was extremely angry when he found his plans had been completely destroyed. But we are hopeful, we work hard, and hope that we may yet be able to support ourselves comfortably without aid from any one. We are young, we are strong, we trust each other, and have a firm faith in our success.

"I had only one regret in leaving Europe, and that was that my faithful friend, the noble and devoted invisible dog, was obliged to remain on the other side of the Atlantic. Why this was so I do not know, but perhaps it was for the best. I never told my wife of his existence, and if she had accidentally discovered it, I know not what might have been the effects upon her nervous system.

"The dog accompanied me through Austria, Switzerland, and France to Havre, from which port we sailed. I took leave of him on the gang-plank. He licked my hands, and I caressed and stroked him. People might have thought that my actions denoted insanity, but every one was so greatly occupied in these last moments before departure, that perhaps I was not noticed. Just as I left him and hastened on board, a sailor fell overboard from the gang-plank. He was quickly rescued, but could not imagine why he had fallen. I believe, however, that he was tripped up by the snake part of my friend as he convulsively rushed away."

The young man ceased, and gazed pensively upon the floor.

" Well, well, well! " exclaimed Aunt Martha, "if those are the sort of experiences you had, I don't wonder that Realism was wonderful enough for you. The invisible creature was very good to you, I am sure, but I am glad it did not come with you to America."

David, who had been waiting for an opportunity to speak, now interrupted further comments by stating that it was daylight, and if I thought well of it, he would open the window-shutters, so that we might see any one going toward the town. A milkman, he said, passed the house very early every morning. When the shutters were opened we were all amazed that the night should have passed so quickly.

The tall burglar and the young man now began to exhibit a good deal of anxiety.

" I should like very much to know,"
said the former, " what you intend to do
in regard to us. It cannot be that you
think of placing that young gentleman
and myself in the hands of the law. Of
course, this man," pointing to the stout
burglar, " cannot expect anything but a
just punishment of his crimes; but after
what we have told you, you must certainly
be convinced that our connection with the
affair is entirely blameless, and should be
considered as a piece of very bad luck."

" That," said I, " is a matter which will
receive all the consideration it needs."

At this moment David announced the
milkman. Counselling my man to keep
strict guard over the prisoners, I went
out to the road, stopped the milkman, and
gave him a message which I was certain
would insure the prompt arrival at my
house of sufficient force to take safe charge
of the burglars. Excited with the importance of the commission, he whipped up
his horse and dashed away.

When I returned to the house I besought
my wife and Aunt Martha to go to bed,
that they might yet get some hours of
sleep; but both refused. They did not feel
in the least like sleep, and there was a

subject on which they wished to consult with me in the dining-room.

"Now," said Aunt Martha, when the door had been closed, "these men have freely told us their stories; whether they are entirely true or not, must, of course, be a matter of opinion; but they have laid their cases before us, and we should not place them all in the hands of the officers of the law without giving them due consideration, and arriving at a decision which shall be satisfactory to ourselves."

"Let us take them in order," said I. "What do you think of the tall man's case?"

"I think he is a thief and manufacturer of falsehoods," said my wife promptly.

"I am afraid," said Aunt Martha, "that he is not altogether innocent; but there is one thing greatly in his favour, — when he told of the feelings which overcame him when he saw that little child sleeping peacefully in its bed in the house which he had unintentionally robbed, I felt there must be good points in that man's nature. What do you think of him?"

"I think he is worst of the lot," I answered, "and as there are now two votes against him, he must go to the lock-up.

And now what of the stout fellow?" I asked.

"Oh, he is a burglar by his own confession," said my wife; "there can be no doubt of that."

"I am afraid you are right," said Aunt Martha.

"I know she is," said I, "and James Barlow, or whatever his name may be, shall be delivered to the constable."

"Of course, there can be no difference of opinion in regard to the young man," said Aunt Martha quickly. "Both the others admitted that he had nothing to do with this affair except as a journalist, and although I do not think he ought to get his realistic ideas in that way, I would consider it positively wicked to send him into court in company with those other men. Consider the position in which he would be placed before the world. Consider his young wife."

"I cannot say," said my wife, "that I am inclined to believe all parts of his story."

"I suppose," said I, laughing, "that you particularly refer to the invisible dog-snake."

"I'm not so sure about all that," she answered. "Since the labours of the psychic researchers began, we have heard of a great many strange things; but it is evident that he is a young man of education and culture, and in all probability a journalist or literary man. I do not think he should be sent to the lock-up with common criminals."

"There!" cried Aunt Martha, "two in his favour. He must be released. It's a poor rule that does not work both ways."

I stood for a few moments undecided. If left to myself, I would have sent the trio to the county town, where, if any one of them could prove his innocence, he could do so before the constitutional authorities; but having submitted the matter to my wife and aunt, I could not well override their decision. As for what the young man said, I gave it no weight whatever, for of course he would say the best he could for himself. But the testimony of the others had weight. When they both declared that he was not a burglar, but merely a journalist, engaged in what he supposed to be his duty, it would seem to be a cruel thing to stamp him as a criminal by putting him in charge of the constables.

But my indecision soon came to an end, for Aunt Martha declared that no time should be lost in setting the young man free, for should the people in town arrive and see him sitting bound with the others it would ruin his character forever. My wife agreed.

"Whatever there may be of truth in his story," she said, "one of two things is certain, — either he has had most wonderful experiences out of which he may construct realistic novels which will give him fortune and reputation, or he has a startling imagination, which, if used in the production of works in the romantic school, will be of the same advantage to his future. Looking upon it, even in this light and without any reference to his family and the possible effects on his own moral nature, we shall assume a great responsibility in deliberately subjecting such a person to criminal prosecution and perhaps conviction."

This was enough. "Well," said I, "we will release the young fellow and send the two other rascals to jail."

"That was not well expressed," said my wife, "but we will not criticise words at present."

We returned to the library and I announced my decision. When he heard it the stout burglar exhibited no emotion.

His expression indicated that, having been caught, he expected to be sent to jail, and that was the end of it. Perhaps he had been through this experience so often that he had become used to it. The tall man, however, took the announcement in a very different way. His face grew dark and his eyes glittered. "You are making a great mistake," he said to me, "a very great mistake, and you will have to bear the consequences."

"Very good," said I, "I will remember that remark when your trial comes on."

The behaviour of the young man was unexceptional. He looked upon us with a face full of happy gratitude, and, as he thanked us for the kind favour and the justice which we had shown him, his eyes seemed dim with tears. Aunt Martha was much affected.

"I wonder if his mother is living," she whispered to me. "A wife is a great deal, but a mother is more. If I had thought of her sooner I would have spoken more strongly in his favour. And now you should untie him at once and let him go home. His wife must be getting terribly anxious."

The young man overheard this last remark.

" You will confer a great favour on me, sir," he said, " if you will let me depart as soon as possible. I feel a great repugnance to be seen in company with these men, as you may imagine, from wearing a mask on coming here. If I leave immediately I think I can catch the first train from your station."

I considered the situation. If I did what I was asked, there would be two bound burglars to guard, three women and a child to protect, an uncertain stranger at liberty, and only David and myself to attend to the whole business. " No, sir," said I, " I shall not untie you until the officers I sent for are near at hand; then I will release you, and you can leave the house by the back way without being seen by them. There are other morning trains which will take you into the city early enough."

" I think you are a little hard on him," remarked Aunt Martha, but the young man made no complaint.

" I will trust myself to you, sir," he said.

The officers arrived much sooner than I expected. There were five of them, including the Chief of Police, and they were accompanied by several volunteer assistants, among whom was the milkman who had been my messenger. This morning his customers might wait for their milk, for all business must give way before such an important piece of sightseeing as this.

I had barely time to untie the young man and take him to the back of the house before the officers and their followers had entered the front door. There was now a great deal of questioning, a great deal of explanation, a great deal of discussion as to whether my way of catching burglars was advisable or not, and a good deal of talk about the best method of taking the men to town. Some of the officers were in favour of releasing the two men, and then deciding in what manner they should be taken to town ; and if this plan had been adopted, I believe that these two alert and practical rascals would have taken themselves out of my house without the assistance of the officers, or at least would have caused a great deal of trouble and perhaps injury in endeavouring to do so.

But the Chief of Police was of my mind, and before the men were entirely released from the ropes by which I had tied them, they were securely manacled.

A requisition made on David and myself

to appear as witnesses, the two men were taken from the house to the wagons in which the officers and their followers had come.   My wife and Aunt Martha had gone upstairs before the arrival of the police, and were watching the outside proceeding from a window.

Standing in the hallway, I glanced into the dining-room, and was surprised to see the young man still standing by a side door. I had thought him gone, but perhaps it was wise in him to remain, and not show himself upon the road until the coast was entirely clear. He did not see me, and was looking backward into the kitchen, a cheerful and animated expression upon his face. This expression did not strike me pleasantly. He had escaped a great danger, it was true, but it was no reason for this rather obtrusive air of exultation. Just then Alice came into the dining-room from the kitchen, and the young man stepped back, so that she did not notice him. As she passed he gently threw his arm quietly around her neck and kissed her.

At that very instant, even before the girl had time to exclaim, in rushed David from the outer side door.

" I've been watching you, you rascal," he shouted; " you're done for now ! " and he threw his strong arms around the man, pinioning his arms to his side.

The young fellow gave a great jerk, and began to struggle powerfully. His face turned black with rage ; he swore, he kicked. He made the most frenzied efforts to free himself, but David's arms were strong, his soul was full of jealous fury, and in a moment I had come to his assistance. Each of us taking the young fellow by an arm, we ran him into the hallway and out of the front door, Alice aiding us greatly by putting her hands against the man's back and pushing most forcibly.

" Here's another one," cried David. " I'll appear against him. He's the worst of the lot."

Without knowing what it all meant, the Chief clapped the nippers on our prisoner, justly believing that if burglars were about to show themselves so unexpectedly, the best thing to do was to handcuff them as fast as they appeared, and then to ask questions. The reasons for not having produced this man before, and for producing him now, were not very satisfactory to the officer.

"Have you any more in the cellar?" he asked. "If so, I should like to take a look at them before I start away."

At this moment Aunt Martha made her appearance at the front door.

"What are you going to do with that young man?" she asked sharply. "What right have you to put irons upon him?"

"Aunt Martha," said I, stepping back to her, "what do you think he has done?"

"I don't know," said she; "how should I know? All I know is that we agreed to set him free."

I addressed her solemnly: "David and I believe him to be utterly depraved. He availed himself of the first moments of his liberation to kiss Alice." Aunt Martha looked at me with wide-open eyes, and then her brows contracted.

"He did, did he?" said she. "And that is the kind of a man he is. Very good. Let him go to jail with the others. I don't believe one word about his young wife. If kissing respectable young women is the way he studies Realism the quicker he goes to jail the better," and with that she walked into the house.

When the men had been placed in the two vehicles in which the police had come,

the Chief and I made an examination of
the premises, and we found that the house
had been entered by a kitchen window, in
exactly the manner which the tall burglar
had described.   Outside of this window,
close to the wall, we found a leathern bag,
containing what the Chief declared to be
an excellent assortment of burglars' tools.
The officers and their prisoners now drove
away, and we were left to a long morning
nap, if we were so fortunate as to get it,
and a late breakfast.

In the course of the trial of the three
men who had entered my house some interesting points in regard to them were
brought out.   Several detectives and po-
licemen from New York were present, and
their testimony proved that my three burglars were men of eminence in their profession, and that which most puzzled the
metropolitan detectives was to discover
why these men should have been willing
to devote their high talents to the comparatively insignificant business of breaking into a suburban dwelling.

The tall man occupied a position of
peculiar eminence in criminal circles.   He
was what might be called a criminal manager.   He would take contracts for the

successful execution of certain crimes, —
bank robberies, for instance, — and while
seldom taking part in the actual work of a
burglary or similar operation, he would
plan all the details of the affair, and select
and direct his agents with great skill
and judgment. He had never been arrested before, and the detectives were delighted, believing they would now have an
opportunity of tracing to him a series of
very important criminal operations that
had taken place in New York and some
other large cities. He was known as
Lewis Mandit, and this was believed to
be his real name.

The stout man was a first-class professional burglar and nothing more, and was
in the employ of Mandit. The young man
was a decidedly uncommon personage.
He was of a good family, had been educated at one of our principal colleges, had
travelled, and was in every way qualified
to make a figure in society. He had been
a newspaper man, and a writer for leading
periodicals, and had shown considerable
literary ability; but a life of honest indus-
try did not suit his tastes, and he had now
adopted knavery as a regular profession.

This man, who was known among his

present associates as Sparky, still showed himself occasionally in newspaper offices, and was generally supposed to be a correspondent for a Western journal; but his real business position was that of Mandit's head man.

Sparky was an expert in many branches of crime. He was an excellent forger, a skilful lock-picker, an ingenious planner of shady projects, and had given a great deal of earnest study to the subject of the loopholes of the law. He had a high reputation in criminal circles for his ability in getting his fellow-rascals out of jail. There was reason to believe that in the past year no less than nine men, some condemned to terms of imprisonment, and some held for trial, had escaped by means of assistance given them by Sparky.

His methods of giving help to jail-birds were various. Sometimes liberty was conferred through the agency of saws and ropes, at other times through that of a habeas corpus and an incontestible alibi. His means were adapted to the circumstances of the case, and it was believed that if Sparky could be induced to take up the case of a captured rogue, the man had better chance of finding himself free than the law had of keeping him behind bars, especially if his case were treated before it had passed into its more chronic stages.

Sparky's success was greatly due to his extremely specious manner, and his power of playing the part that the occasion demanded. In this particular he was even the superior of Mandit, who was an adept in this line. These two men found no difficulty in securing the services of proficient burglars, safe-robbers, and the like ; for, in addition to the high rewards paid these men, they were in a manner insured against permanent imprisonment in case of misfortune. It was always arranged that, if any of their enterprises came to grief, and if either Mandit or Sparky should happen to be arrested, the working miscreants should substantiate any story their superiors might choose to tell of themselves, and, if necessary, to take upon themselves the whole responsibility of the crime. In this case their speedy release was to be looked upon as assured.

A great deal of evidence in regard to the character and practices of these two men came from the stout burglar, commonly known as Barney Fitch. When he found that nothing was to be expected from his two astute employers, and that they were in as bad a place as himself, he promptly turned State's evidence, and told all that he knew about them.

It was through the testimony of this man that the motive for the attempted robbery of my house was found out. It had no connection whatever with the other burglaries of our neighbourhood, those, probably, having been committed by low-class thieves, who had not broken into my house simply because my doors and windows had been so well secured; nor had our boy, George William, any share whatever in the protection of the household.

The burglary was undertaken solely for the purpose of getting possession of some important law papers, which were to be used in a case in which I was concerned, which soon would be tried. If these papers could be secured by the opposite party, the side on which I was engaged would have no case at all, and a suit involving a great deal of property must drop. With this end in view the unscrupulous defendants in the case had employed Mandit to procure the papers; and that astute criminal manager had not only arranged all the details of the affair, but had gone himself to the scene of action in order to see that there should be no mistake in carrying out the details of this most important piece of business.

The premises had been thoroughly reconnoitred by Sparky, who, a few days before the time fixed for the burglary, had visited my house in the capacity of an agent of a telescopic bookcase, which could be extended as new volumes were required, therefore need never exhibit empty shelves. The young man had been included in the party on account of his familiarity with legal documents, it being, of course, of paramount importance that the right papers should be secured. His ingenuity was also to be used to cover up, if possible, all evidence that the house had been entered at all, it being desirable to make it appear to the court that I had never had these documents in my possession, and that they never existed.

Had it not been for a very natural desire for refreshment that interfered with their admirably laid plans, it is probable that the mechanical skill of Mandit would have been equal to the noiseless straightening of the bent bolt, and the obliteration of the scratches and dents made by the attempts upon other shutters, and that Sparky, after relocking all open desks or cabinets, and after the exit of the others, would have closed and fastened the kitchen shutters, and would then have left the house by means of an open window in the upper hall and the roof of a piazza.

Thus it was that these three men, so eminent in their different spheres of earnest endeavour, came to visit my comparatively humble abode; and thus it was that they not only came to that abode, but to the deepest grief. They were "wanted" in so many quarters, and on so many charges, that before they had finished serving out their various sentences their ability to wickedly avail themselves of the property of others would have suffered greatly from disuse, and the period of life left them for the further exercise of those abilities would be inconveniently limited.

I was assured by a prominent detective that it had been a long time since two such dangerous criminals as Mandit and Sparky had fallen into the hands of the law. These men, by means of very competent outside assistance, made a stout fight for acquittal on some of the charges brought against them; but when they found that further effort of this kind would be unavailing, and that they would be sentenced to long terms of imprisonment, they threw off their masks of outraged probity and stood out in their true characters of violent and brutal ruffians. Barney Fitch, the cracksman, was a senior warden compared to them.

It was a long time before my Aunt Martha recovered from her disappointment in regard to the youngest burglar.

"Of course I was mistaken," she said. "That sort of thing will happen; but I really had good grounds for believing him to be a truthful person, so I am not ashamed for having taken him for what he said he was. I have now no doubt before he fell in his wicked ways that he was a very good writer, and might have become a novelist or a magazine author; but his case is a very sad proof that the study of Realism may be carried too far," and she heaved a sigh.

THE END.